Books by TLW Savage

First Test Hexology (Six books)

Alex Twice Abducted

Alex Terrified Hero

Alex Inner Voice

Alex String Sword

Alex & Hheilea Challenge the Darkness

Alex & the Crystal of Jedh...coming soon

Heroes come in all sizes

Tuffy

Pooh and P'Nut

Pooh and Eeyore

Pronunciations
And Definitions

- **Anhedonic** –

    Anhedonic is a psychological term that refers to the inability or reduced ability to experience pleasure or joy.

- **Anthropomorphize** –

    Anthropomorphize is the attributing of human characteristics, feelings, or behavior to an animal or to anything.

- **Annie** –

    Annie is a very loving and friendly dog. Her breed is Newfie or Newfoundland. She is very big. They have webbed toes and are very strong swimmers.

- **Artificial Intelligence** –

    Artificial Intelligence (AI) is a set of technologies allowing computers to perform a number of things. In some ways, it makes the computers seem intelligent, but they are still just programs doing what they've been designed to do. As the artificial intelligence gets better, it is harder to tell the difference between the artificial intelligence and real intelligence.

- **Braying** –

    Braying is one of the sounds that donkeys make.

- **Caressed** –

    Caressed is to touch or stroke lovingly.

- **Deterministic Laws –**

    Deterministic Laws are rules that dictate that a system's current state completely determines its future state. Basically, they mean everything can be figured out if you have enough starting information. They were wrong.

- **Detritus –**

    Detritus is a fancy word for dead stuff including sticks, branches, dead plants, or debris of any kind.

- **Dusk –**

    The time of fading light after the sun has set.

- **Electromagnetic Pulse (EMP) –**

    A brief burst of electromagnetic energy that can damage or destroy electronic devices.

- **Eeyore** –Ē ôr – This sounds like the letter E followed by the word ore.

    He is a chubby donkey and a main character in this story.

- **Faith –**

    Faith is belief in something that is unprovable or a complete trust in someone or something. Faith is also the wrapping paper that keeps our hope safe.

- **Forbearance**

    Forbearance is a patient self-control: restraint and tolerance.

- **Fuego** – Fuā gō

    He is a very temperamental hummingbird and only 3 inches long. He is a Calliope hummingbird.

- **Globules –**

    Globules are small round particles or a balls of a substance such as water.

- **Hubbub –**

    Hubbub is a chaotic noisy situation.

- **Intersection –**

    An intersection is where two or more things, such as roads, cross or meet.

- **Izzy or Isabella –** Iz ē

    She is a human eighteen-year-old, and she is an former classmate of Noah's.

- **Laws of Physics –**

    Physics is full of laws describing all kinds of fun, amazing, and, sometimes, dangerous things. Newton's Law of Motion is one example describing how objects move, but it doesn't cover how things move in quantum physics.

- **Magnetism –**

    Magnetism is the natural phenomenon or force that can attract or repel other magnets. There is much more about magnetism, but this is a simple explanation.

- **Marmots –**

    Marmots are heavily built burrowing rodents. They typically live in mountainous locations.

- **Noah –** No-uh

    He is a nerd. He is more at ease with animals than with humans.

- **NGOs –**

    Non-governmental organizations have no fixed or formal definition. They are generally defined as nonprofit entities independent of governmental influence or control, but they may receive government funding.

- **Physics –**

    Physics is the branch of science involved in the study of energy, and the study of the very small things that make up everything. This is a simplified definition. There is much more to physics.

- **Pika –**

    Pikas are small mammals that look like seven-inch-long rabbits. They are very interesting creatures.

- **P'Nut –** P ē Nut

    P'Nut is an eastern gray squirrel. He loves watching movies with his friends and has dreams of being a superhero.

- **Pooh –** Pu

    Pooh is a black bear. He is only about nine months old. He is light brown and likes wearing a ragged red shirt just like the fictional bear, Winnie the Pooh.

- **Quantum –**

    A simple definition of quantum used in this book is that quantum is referring to both the study of how matter and energy function at the atomic and subatomic levels, and quantum is referring to those very strange ways matter and energy function at the atomic and subatomic levels. How things act at the quantum level both determine our reality and are responsible for some very strange things that hardly seem real. It is really mind-bending stuff and has done amazing things for us with new technology.

- **Superposition –**

    This is hard stuff, but the use of it in this book means being able to change reality using science. The quantum state of superposition is the normal unexamined state of particles. When we examine the quantum state of superposition, we change reality.

- **Sardinian Donkey –**

    The Sardinian Donkey is an Italian breed of donkey. They are gray. A full grown one is generally about 40 inches tall at the withers, lying at the base of the neck just above the shoulders.

- **Self-deprecation –**

    Being modest about yourself or criticizing yourself. In this usage, it means making modest statements about themselves.

- **Splooted –**

    Means for an animal to lie flat on its stomach with its front legs out and its hind legs stretched out behind it. Squirrels don't have many sweat glands. They sploot to cool off.

- **Tapetum lucidum –**
    Tapetum lucidum is the reflective layer in the eyes of many animals. It improves night vision by bouncing light back through the retina to the photoreceptors.

- **Tuffy –**

    He is a male, red-tailed hawk, but he was imprinted by bald eagles that accidently adopted him. He thinks he's an eagle.

Pooh and Eeyore

TLW Savage

ISBN-13: 9781947133099

ISBN-10: 1947133099

DEDICATION

This book is dedicated to my fans, Winnie the Pooh lovers, and animal lovers everywhere. My fans enjoyment of my first animal book Tuffy has been a great source of encouragement for me. I am glad that Tuffy and all of his friends have been a great source of entertainment for many. I hope this additional tale about a bear named Pooh, a donkey named Eeyore, and their friends will be that and more for you. Thank you.

I also dedicate this book to my wonderful wife, Debbie, whose forbearance for years with my writing struggles allowed for the opportunity to continue to fruition. All of your support and belief in me and in this project has been instrumental in its success.

What follows is the best thanks I can give. Please read on. Laugh, cry, and think. Be amazed and fascinated. Enjoy, and at the end of the book, have a good life. I love you.

CONTENTS CHAPTER

TL Walker

Prelude
Pooh and Eeyore

Pooh

In 1925, A. A. Milne and E. H. Shepard created the wonderful *Winnie the Pooh*. In years gone by, I and others have enjoyed their creation. Also, I have been inspired by their characterization of Pooh. In my own story, I refer to another fictional bear as Pooh. This bear has some resemblance to the original bear, but only some. I hope this bear, my Pooh, also connects to you, and you enjoy him and his story as much as I did in creating them for you.

Eeyore

Eeyore is another character from the *Winnie the Pooh* books. He is pessimistic, depressed, and anhedonic. In real life, many of us can be pessimistic, depressed, and even anhedonic. Those are serious problems. In the original works of the above artists, Eeyore's friends do try and help him, but they are never successful. It can be very hard to help a friend. It helps immensely if the individual, who has a problem, recognizes the problem and wants to be helped. I hope how Eeyore and his friends deal with his problems is an encouragement to you.

I hope you enjoy reading this story as much or more than I enjoyed creating it for you.

Chapter One

Eeyore

As of 2006, donkeys have been bred into about 185 different breeds. One breed is the Sardinian dwarf donkey. It is, on average, shorter than three feet tall at its shoulders, otherwise called the withers.

Donkeys have much better senses of hearing and smell than humans. They also have a very strong sense of self-preservation. This can make them seem to be stubborn. Also, donkeys, just like humans and other animals, can have serious depression problems.

Donkeys can, like humans, look at something with both eyes or, unlike humans, they can also look at separate things with each eye. Isn't that strange? The world is full of strange and mysterious things.

Eeyore lived in a pasture. As pastures went, it wasn't very good. He rather thought it should have less grass and more thistles. There were thistles along the road in front of the pasture, but the gate was shut, and no one ever came to open the gate, check on him, or take care of him. Eeyore was stuck in a bad pasture of grass. At least it had an old, half-broken down barn and even a small, rickety shed.

An almost full moon shined from the night sky. If anyone else had been there, they would've seen how the moonlight made the gray donkey's gray hair shine. When Eeyore looked up at the night sky, a curl of hair showed, hanging from his forehead.

Between his shiny white-gray coat of hair, his big dark eyes, and the curl of hair, Eeyore would've looked very cute to anyone looking at him. Unfortunately though, Eeyore normally stood with his head bowed toward the ground. With his head hanging down, his big, floppy ears hung almost to the ground.

Up to this point, his life had been very boring except for one terrible, terrible day. Eeyore really didn't have any reason to be happy or cheerful.

The little donkey looked up at the Moon. *It helps me to see, but some clouds are coming. They'll probably cover it up.* He heard a voice from down by his hooves. It startled Eeyore out of his own thoughts. He didn't get very many visitors.

"Hello."

Eeyore looked down. A mouse stood on a stick and looked up at him. Eeyore answered, "Hello."

The mouse asked, "Why do you always look down?"

"I'm talking to you, and you are down. Where do you expect me to look?"

The mouse said, "I've seen you many times in this pasture. I've called out to you before, but this is the first time you've answered me. Others in the area have tried to talk to you, but you don't answer very many times. Almost always, your head hangs down. What's wrong?"

Eeyore stared at the mouse. What the mouse had said was the longest bit of conversation the donkey had heard from anyone. "Why shouldn't my head hang down?"

She answered, "Why? That's silly. There are so many things you won't see with your head hanging down. Plus, it always makes you look sad."

Eeyore thought about what the mouse said before answering, "But I always am sad."

"Wow, that's terrible. I think you need some friends. There are lots of others in this area. You should talk to them." After a pause, the mouse added. "I think you should get away from here and go exploring."

The little donkey stepped back when the mouse said, "That's terrible."

Eeyore answered the mouse, "I can't go exploring."

The mouse shrugged. "You really need a friend. I'd stay and talk, but there's a storm coming, and I have to check on my friends. They might need help. Maybe I'll come back." Before she left, the mouse repeated, "I really think you need some friends."

Eeyore watched the mouse jump off the stick and run into a bush growing in the fence. *What's a friend?* Eeyore considered what the mouse had said. *Friends help each other.* He looked up at the sky. Clouds raced across the sky. *They'll cover up the Moon, but it's setting. Soon, it will be a new day. There's probably going to be a bad storm.* The sad, little donkey shuddered at the memory of another bad storm.

The little donkey looked back at the bush. *I hope that mouse is okay. If only I knew what I could do to help her and her friends.* Eeyore felt something he hadn't noticed before. He felt lonely. *I hope the mouse comes back, but it probably won't.*

The storm came shortly after sunrise. At first, Eeyore took shelter in the very old and leaning barn. He stopped just inside the door. He'd always expected it would fall down at any moment. It had been a good home for Eeyore. When the first big gust hit, Eeyore'd heard the snaps of things breaking above him, and the old barn had groaned.

Eeyore ran out just before the old barn collapsed with a crash. In the horrible wind and debris blowing past, Eeyore barely made it to the only other building in the pasture.

He took shelter in his new home, the very small and rickety shed.

Eeyore barely fit.

The small donkey looked to his right and to his left. Eeyore did this at the same time. He nodded his head. His stomach stuck out on both sides. *I'm getting fat. Well, I guess that comes of not eating enough thistles.*

Above him, the new home Eeyore had taken shelter in shook from a blast of wind. The little donkey looked at the roof of the shed. It wasn't much better than a shed made of sticks. *I don't think it is going to last much longer. I'm surprised it has lasted this long. I should leave, but it's probably just as dangerous outside.* Eeyore looked outside. Leaves, small branches, birds, and other odd things blew past. Something caught his attention. Eeyore looked again. It couldn't have been what he thought it was. It looked like a small piglet had blown past.

At least my fat will make me heavier. I shouldn't blow away, but you never know. I expect something just as bad will happen. Still, I should try. Of course, I deserve all my bad luck.

Eeyore slowly stepped out into the storm. He heard thunder rumbling. At the sound, Eeyore shivered in terror. *I'm going to die.* He flinched from a faint flash of light. *Which way should I go? It probably doesn't make any difference. Any direction I take will be bad.* Eeyore had always wanted to go out on the road, but the gate had kept him in. He wanted to leave the skeletons and the memories.

I'll step behind the big log. It will shelter me, and I can think out of the wind about what to do. Eeyore saw the bush by the fence.

That little mouse. I don't think the bush will give it enough protection. Eeyore looked at the safety of the log and looked at the exposed bush in the fence.

Eeyore turned from the safety of the log. He looked at the ground. Big branches lay in his way. *I don't think I can make it through this mess.* Eeyore tripped and tumbled.

He landed in front of the bush. Over the storm, Eeyore heard a crash behind him. Sticks from his new home blew past. One, it must've been big, hit his rump. Eeyore winced at the pain, but he stayed in front of the bush. "I hope you're okay in there."

Some of the sticks blew over him. *There goes my new home. I probably broke something when I fell.*

Eeyore slowly stood up. His head hung low. Nothing hurt. *It will probably hurt later.* He heard another, bigger crash. Rays of sunlight broke through the dissipating storm. They illuminated a tree lying on the smashed gate. *I can go out on the road and eat the thistles growing along it, but they'll probably give me an upset stomach. The thistles will at least keep me going until I find a new home. Though that home probably won't last either.*

A beautiful double rainbow shined brightly behind the road. *They don't last very long.*

"Little mouse, if you can hear me, I'm leaving to find a new home. I guess this might qualify as the adventure you suggested. I hope you're okay. Thanks for talking to me."

Eeyore waited. He hoped to hear a reply, but none came. With his head hanging low, Eeyore slowly walked away from the only home he'd known. Eeyore left behind the skeletons, but the memories followed.

With the memories, he carried his guilt. *It was my fault. I should've died instead of them.* He traveled down the level straight path of what had been a road. Eeyore couldn't remember when the road hadn't had weeds growing on it. In places, pavement showed through a covering of weeds, leaves, needles, and sticks.

Eeyore felt something hit his rump near his new sore spot. He lashed out with both hind hooves. They didn't hit anything.

The little, lonely donkey continued to walk along the road. *This is probably a bad idea, but I should try to find a new home. I'll walk*

8

along this road. I probably won't find anything suitable, but I need to try.

Eeyore looked back. "Bye, Mom. I'm going to keep trying."

The little, fat donkey turned around. His head hung even lower than it normally hung. The ends of his long, floppy ears gently brushed the ground. He plodded away from the only home he'd ever known.

Chapter Two

A Team is Made

Animals are amazing, but with time and effort most of us can understand why, how, and what they do. Physics is even more mind-bending. Most of us don't have a clue how the laws of physics work. We just have faith that our understanding doesn't matter. Everything still works as it should.

Faith is trust in what we don't know and can't or don't understand. Faith is the wrapping paper that keeps our hope wrapped up safe for us. Life can be tough, but have faith. Keep hope alive. Keep your faith. Do what you can for others, especially those carrying burdens.

Pooh stared at his paw again. Even in the light of the setting sun, he could tell there wasn't any honey left. His nose agreed. Everyone that ate things like honey had appreciated Pooh sharing. The golden-brown, black bear's stomach grumbled a complaint. The problem was there hadn't been any left for the little bear. Pooh remembered where the honey came from. He looked back toward the lake at the honey tree. *After losing so many bees, they need all the honey they have.* He muttered to himself, "Oh, bother."

The little bear, wearing a ragged, red shirt, looked again at the green, succulent plants surrounding him and went back to filling his belly with plants instead of honey. Beside him, a tree trunk rose at an angle to join with the giant tree beside them. That tree towered over everything else in the area. Pooh looked up at the sound of the billie goats returning. They had been sent to retrieve Izzy's backpack and bag. Pooh looked at the young black woman. Her frizzy black hair bobbed on her shoulders.

Izzy said, "Thank you," as the billie goats dropped the bag and backpack.

Annie, the big black dog, walked over and sniffed at the bag. "I'm hungry. I could use some of my food."

One of the goats said, "Sorry we took so long. This one is heavy."

The athletic young woman quickly dug into the backpack. In a voice filled with gratitude, Izzy said, "Food! I'm so hungry. Thank you for your effort. Annie, I'll get you some of your food, too."

"We didn't do much. The nannies did much more during the battle."

Their self-deprecation ended when one of the billies said, "I carried your heavy bag the farthest."

The other billie shook his horns at the other goat. "I carried it up the ridge. You only carried it on the easy slopes."

The two of them pushed, shoved, and butted each other. They trampled over the vegetation Pooh wanted to eat. Pooh yelled at them. "Hey, you're ruining my dinner."

The billies moved their fight away from Pooh. The little bear shook his head at the silly animals and went back to eating. *These plants aren't as good as honey, but I agree with Izzy. I'm hungry, and I could use a nap.*

Owl flew up. "Well, I say now. Izzy has her stuff. Your enemies have been defeated. I think we should show you the options for continuing your journey."

P'Nut, the eastern gray squirrel, said, "Good. We need to go. We need to go. You said there are slides and tunnels?"

One of the furry marmots said, "Yes. One day, I dug a new burrow, and I noticed the big rock in the way crumbled. I learned that I could make burrows much easier, and—"

P'Nut interrupted, "Yes, yes, you already told us all of that. Then, an otter learned of what you could do, and they made you a deal. You already explained that to us. Let's go. Let's go. I need to go get the crystal I hid in the tree."

The little squirrel leapt on a trunk. P'Nut raced up it and into the giant tree.

A bird with a red crest spoke from the side of a different tree trunk it clung to. "You left a crystal in the tree?"

The squirrel had already leapt onto a tree branch far above the ground. "Yes. It's very important."

"It's purple?"

P'Nut said, "Yes, it is. Did you see it?"

"I saw a weasel dragging a purple crystal away during the battle."

"Oh, no! I'll be right back." The squirrel raced into the depths of the tree.

Owl said, "Well, well. It seems like we have a thief to find."

Another animal spoke up. "I was wondering about that creature. It didn't seem to be from around here." A red fox jumped up onto a white and black speckled boulder. "Mr. Pileated Woodpecker, could you show me where you last saw this weasel?"

The big woodpecker pushed off the trunk and took wing. "Follow me. It isn't far."

The fox jumped after it.

P'Nut's voice came from above. "It's gone."

Izzy looked up from putting Annie's food away. "How did that crystal get back here?"

P'Nut's rapid fire voice answered, growing louder as he came closer. "This is bad. This is bad. It's a long story. I was supposed to help keep it safe. I thought it was safe. What can I do?"

The owl said, "A fox is after the thief."

At that moment, the big woodpecker flew back. "Come with me." It turned and flew away. "The fox is on the trail and has already found something bad."

Annie wolfed down the food Izzy had poured out for her. Everyone else followed after as best as they could. Pooh really just wanted to take a nap. It had been a very long day.

He valiantly ignored his sore paws and hurried after the other animals and Izzy. Pooh always smelled the currents of the air. As he climbed over boulders, past flowers, and through bushes, Pooh smelled something bad. "Coyote, I smell wolf."

From just ahead, the fox answered. "You're right. It appears that the weasel met up with a wolf, and they continued on together."

The fox quickly followed the trail. Otter spoke up. "They're headed to the slide."

Pooh asked, "What's the slide?"

P'Nut interjected, "They already told us about the slide."

The otter explained, "At first, we worked with the marmots to just make slides locally, but we decided to connect tunnels and slides to carry us down to the big lake. It is amazing. Although, it does take a very long time to hike back up. If I didn't have other things I need to do, I'd go down the slide almost every day."

P'Nut said, "Everyone, hurry up. They're getting away."

Owl spoke from above. "The other animals learned about it and talked to me. We made the decision to increase the slide's size. Even a bear can use it now to go to the lower elevations."

The beaver, Stump, said, "If you're going on a slide, you'll be going lower. Remember, after a storm like this, there can be flash flooding below."

A marmot said, "Many of the animals are talking about wintering down by the big lake. One of us marmots decided to make a new burrow area for his colony. He stumbled into a limestone cave. We've made a new tunnel and slide that runs south and —"

At the word "south," Izzy interrupted, "That's the direction I need to go. I'm supposed to take Annie to Noah, but we should help recover the crystal first. It should be taken to Noah."

P'Nut said, "Yes, we need to take the south route after we get the crystal back. Move faster. Move faster."

The otter said, "Those plans to winter down by the big lake need to be reconsidered. There's some bad danger there. It's worse the closer to the big lake you get."

Owl said, "Am I correct in assuming that going south will get you to safety?"

Izzy answered, "Yes. Annie will be safe, and she'll get training to help her control gravity."

Coyote said, "Pooh, I think you should go with them."

Pooh stopped with his mouth open, ready to bite into a plant. "Me? I don't think so. Why me?"

Coyote said, "Pooh, you are very special. Someday, if I ever have pups, I'll tell them I knew the great Pooh when he was just a silly little bear. This training would be great for you. You've got the ability

14

to be a great friend to many."

A thought surprised Pooh. "What about you, Coyote? You could come with me."

"Me?" Coyote sat. "I'm just a trickster."

Pooh looked at Coyote and, then, at the other departing animals. "You're more than that."

"You haven't left yet, and you never know when a trickster might show up."

Pooh heard a shout.

"Someone broke the Meeting Agreement."

Owl's voice carried back to them. "Well, well, this is bad."

Pooh came around a tree. The animals stood gathered around a bare patch of ground. A shivering rabbit stood right in the middle. Pooh heard the creature's pitiful voice.

"My brother and I were eating some fern leaves when it happened. A wolf came up carrying something in its mouth. A weasel jumped down off the wolf and attacked my brother. It was horrible."

Owl said, "Well, well, we can't have this. Where did they go?"

"After they ate my brother, they went down the slide."

P'Nut ran up. "Where's the slide?"

Owl interrupted, "STOP!"

Everyone looked at Owl. Even P'Nut stood still. The little squirrel only shifted from foot to foot a little. Pooh looked at Owl. *This isn't what I expected from the old owl.*

Owl coughed and said, "Ahem. I know, P'Nut, that you are in a hurry, but this is important. Who is going after the thief with this resourceful little squirrel?"

Izzy said, "Annie and I need to go after them."

The crowd parted for them. Annie asked, "Will we be okay?"

"It's very smooth. It dumps you out into a big pool of water at the bottom."

Owl said, "Well, well, very good. Is anyone else going with them? Anyone going with them step forward."

Owl looked right at Pooh.

Pooh felt Coyote pushing against him.

Coyote said, "They'll need your help, and by going with them, you'll get training for your special ability, and I'm not talking about your nose. You're going to be famous."

Pooh said, "I don't want to be famous. I would be happy living up here. I could have lots of friends."

Coyote said, "You'll always have a friend in me although I should warn you. I'm not a very good friend." He pushed Pooh harder. "They need you."

Pooh stumbled forward. "Will I see you again?"

Coyote said, "You never know when trouble will show up."

Owl said, "Okay, P'Nut, you, Annie, Izzy, and Pooh are going on this great adventure to catch the thieves. You need to make a pact, a promise, to catch the thieves, retrieve the stolen crystal, and, more importantly, to help and protect each other."

Izzy asked, "Why do we need this promise?"

Owl ruffled his feathers and stood tall. "Agreements and promises are how we new animals are more than just the wild animals we used to be. We are more. You can be more by working as a team. Are you four ready to enter into this pact?"

The four said, "Yes," although Pooh answered after the others.

"Then repeat after me. 'We promise to catch the thieves, retrieve the stolen crystal, help and protect each other.'"

The four repeated the promise and Izzy said, "Wow. You are quite the owl."

"Yes, I am. Thank you. Now, the biggest should go first. At the bottom of our wonderful slide is a pool. Get out of the way as quickly as you can. Remember, you are chasing a wolf and a weasel. Both of them are nasty creatures. Also, we have heard stories about danger down by the lake. Happy hunting."

P'Nut jumped. "Can we go now? Where's the slide?"

Otter pointed to a big dark hole under a boulder. Without another word, the squirrel jumped into the hole and disappeared.

Owl said, "Well, well, well, he's an impulsive fellow. The rest of you get going."

Pooh looked at the opening to the slide. *Owl just warned us, and Otter said something about trouble by the big lake.* "Coyote, is this the slide that goes to the big lake?"

"Yes, it is."

One after the other, the dog, then Izzy jumped into the hole. Everyone heard Izzy scream. "It's dark in here."

The otter said, "There is one section that is a bit bumpy, but it's fun."

Before he could think anymore, Pooh jumped in the hole. *This is a good story, but I wish there wasn't so much trouble and there was more honey.*

Chapter Three

Wolves See Eeyore

Eeyore was created in 1925 by English author A. A. Milne and English illustrator E. H. Shepard. They created him as a gloomy, depressed, and pessimistic donkey. We all know people with those struggles. Mental illness is real, and it manifests in many ways. People with mental illness can still manage to function in society, but sometimes they fail. Help is available.

Eeyore walked along the road. He stopped only to eat the occasional thistle. It had been a long day. The terrain along the road grew steadily rockier. Eeyore hadn't seen anyone. If Eeyore had lifted his head at the first part of his walk, he would've noticed some buildings, but he went right past them. Eeyore didn't even notice the driveways leading to those buildings, but they didn't look much like driveways. They all had weeds growing in them. Even the road had weeds. The farther Eeyore went, the worse the road was.

He felt a sharp pain on his rump. His tail lashed and his hind hooves kicked out. If something had been there, Eeyore would've smashed it. A big black fly flew away.

I made a bad choice going this way on the road. At least there have been some thistles, but I'll probably get indigestion from them. I wonder where I'm going.

A butterfly fluttered by Eeyore. He lifted his head to look at it. When he did, the blue of a large body of water on his right surprised Eeyore. He stopped. Eeyore stared at the water. *What is this?* He'd

18

never seen such a big body of water. A big bird flew over the water. Eeyore spotted other birds floating on the water. *I haven't been looking for a new home very well. I need to look around more.*

To his left, a hill rose up toward some mountains. Very few trees grew on the hill above him. *This could be a good place to stay, but I don't see any new home.* Eeyore really hoped to find another old barn or shed. Even something built of sticks would be better than nothing. *I wonder if I could build something with sticks.*

He gazed at the hill. More and more trees grew farther away from him. Where the hill reached the base of a mountain, trees covered the hill.

Eeyore spotted a lightning strike over the mountains. He hadn't noticed the black clouds building over the mountains. *I hope that storm doesn't come this way. I don't have any shelter. Oh, well, that's what'll probably happen. I better keep going.*

The donkey looked ahead on the road. Eeyore'd never been to this body of water. In fact, he didn't remember being anywhere other than his field. Eeyore didn't want to think of the time he'd spent as a foal in the field. He didn't want to remember the others. He didn't want to remember his—. Eeyore resumed plodding along. The little donkey looked back at the hill.

Eeyore spotted something. Five wolves ran at an angle down the hill. They would soon cross the road right ahead of him. The five ran in a single file. *Wolves. Oh, well. They've spotted me by now. If they are going to eat me, it's too late. I might as well continue on. Maybe the wolves will get upset stomachs although that won't do me much good.*

If the wolves are going to eat me, I suppose I'll fight them. Eeyore plodded ahead, but he did keep one eye on the approach of the wolves. The wolves were about the same height as the donkey, but the donkey outweighed them.

Eeyore heard the wolves talking.

"I say we should stop and play with the donkey."

"We already ate a deer. I remember you saying you couldn't eat another bite."

"We've been called. We shouldn't stop."

"Stopping for a little time would let our stomachs settle. Mine doesn't feel good after all that food."

"I told you not to stuff yourself so much."

"We're wolves. We always stuff ourselves."

"Yes, but we heard the call. You should've stopped eating."

"You didn't stop eating."

"This isn't about me. You could've stopped first."

The wolves came out onto the road right by Eeyore. The little donkey braced himself for a fight. "I hate to interrupt your argument, but are you going to eat me?"

The wolf in the lead answered, "I'm sorry. We just ate, and we have to get somewhere. Plus, we already have upset stomachs."

The second wolf snarled at Eeyore, "I could take you in three seconds."

The third wolf said, "The donkey with the herd of sheep almost killed you. If we hadn't distracted it, you'd be dead."

The fourth wolf said, "You ran from that other thing. What was it? A llama?"

The fifth wolf, a younger one, said, "Ignore them. They're idiots."

The second wolf said, "That was a big donkey. It would've killed any of us. This one is tiny."

Eeyore said, "I am small, but, sorry, I would fight."

The fifth wolf stopped and asked, "Sorry?"

Eeyore shrugged and said, "It's my nature. I can't help fighting."

The fifth wolf said, "You sound a bit crazy."

The third wolf said, "You hear that. This is a crazy donkey. You don't want to mess with it."

The second wolf said, "I don't care if it's crazy. It's small. I could kill it easy by myself."

Eeyore started to shrug, but he changed his mind and kept plodding along. At a thought, he asked, "Where are you going?"

"We're going to the end of the lake. Another pack has asked for our help."

Eeyore asked, "Do wolf packs help each other?" *Lake? This body of water is called a "lake."*

"Naw, not usually, but these are new and strange times."

Another wolf asked, "Where are you going?"

Eeyore shrugged again. "I'm looking for a new home. I'm going down this road."

"Maybe we'll see you again. That's the direction we're going."

The second wolf said, "Hey, that's great. In a day, we'll be ready for some more food."

The third wolf said, "This crazy donkey would make a rug out of you. You better hope we don't cross paths with it."

The fourth wolf said, "Donkeys are more trouble than they're

21

worth."

The lead wolf hollered, "Enough talking already! Keep going. I want to get to the mouth of the river by early tomorrow morning."

The fifth wolf said, "How much farther are we going?"

"We'll rest at those tall trees ahead of us. A bit of sleep will settle my stomach."

In single file, the wolves trotted along the road and slowly moved ahead of the little donkey.

Eeyore plodded along. He didn't move very fast, but he just kept going. The little donkey considered the wolves stopping for the night ahead of him. *They probably all won't go to sleep. That one is going to try to kill me, but I'll probably fight back. It'll probably kill me. I hope he dies of indigestion.*

The little donkey saw bubbles floating up out of the lake. Each bubble had a green creature in it. The bubbles took the creatures through the air toward the other end of the lake. *That's strange. Those bubbles look like water. The world outside my pasture has so many unusual things. I should've stayed in my pasture. Maybe I could've salvaged some boards and sticks and made a shelter against the log. How were those structures made?*

The little donkey lifted his head. He'd heard some thunder. He shivered in fear at the sound. The storm over the mountains didn't seem to be getting bigger or closer to him. *It will probably come here. I hope the wolves don't sleep too close to those trees. When lightning hits the trees, it could kill them. I'll probably get hit and die, too.* Eeyore shuddered at the memory of another lightning storm and a lightning strike.

The wolves had been running along the road ahead of him, but now they moved toward the trees.

That's a bad idea. Maybe I should warn them. They probably

22

wouldn't listen to me. That might be better. Then they wouldn't be alive to eat me, but something else will probably happen to me. I might as well warn them.

Eeyore kept plodding along. He drew close enough to see the wolves had lain down near the trees. *I thought so. They're too close.*

The donkey kept plodding along. As he drew nearer, he angled slightly toward them. *If they do decide to eat me, they won't have to go so far to get to me. Too bad, I'll fight. Fighting back is probably just useless. It'll make the pain last longer. I hope it will be less painful than dying by a lightning strike.* Again, Eeyore shuddered at the memory of another lightning storm.

The grass on the road muffled the plodding of his hooves. His course took Eeyore straight to a spot of clear pavement. *I could go around it. Maybe they haven't heard me. I could go on past them and not get eaten. Oh, what's the use?*

Eeyore continued straight. The muffled thumps of his hooves changed to a louder and clearer thud, thud, thud, and, sure enough, a voice called out.

"What do we have here?"

The alpha-male wolf said, "Leave the donkey alone. We need our sleep. That little donkey isn't worth the fight, and you're still stuffed from our earlier prey."

"We can take him easy. He'll make a good snack in the morning. There aren't many animals up where we're going, except for those working with her and the few tough ones that survive on their own."

A third voice spoke up from the wolves. "Who said 'we?' You said you could take the donkey by yourself. We're going to watch."

"That's just stupid."

"Oh, saying you're stupid now, are you?"

"No, I—"

"Oh, you're trying to back out of a fight."

"No, I'm not."

At those words, the wolf who'd threatened Eeyore earlier jumped up and charged at the little donkey. "Little donkey, I'm going to kill you."

The wolf lunged for Eeyore's throat. His lips were pulled back which revealed his big, sharp teeth clear down to the red of his gums. Eeyore's hooves moved surprisingly fast. He dodged. Ears back, he thrust his big, blocky head at the wolf. His big mouth opened wide and large, buck teeth flashed in the setting sun.

The wolf realized his danger.

Another wolf yelled, "He's going to bite your ear off."

Another yelled, "If he's lucky, it'll just be his ear."

Eeyore still thought during the fight. *I'm probably going to miss his whole head. It would be nice to at least rip off an ear. It'll make his breakfast worse, but I'll probably miss that, too.*

The pack leader snarled a warning, "Keep the fight quieter."

The wolf did manage to roll his head and dodge the bite. Unfortunately, for the wolf, when his head and body went one way, his tail went the other.

Eeyore lunged forward and clamped his teeth on the wolf's tail.

The wolf let out a howl of pain. "Owwwwww!"

From over by the tall trees, the alpha said, "I said 'keep the fight quieter.' I'm trying to get some sleep. You don't want to bother me. This is my last warning."

24

The wolf twisted around. He snapped at Eeyore's side.

The donkey danced with the wolf's movement. Eeyore tugged on the wolf's tail as he danced. That pulled on the wolf. The snapping teeth missed. Eeyore tugged back and forth with his head. He ground his big incisors into the skin of the wolf's tail.

The wolf snapped at his packmates. "Why don't you attack?"

Eeyore tugged, ground his teeth, and danced. The wolf desperately slashed.

The three wolves watching sat still. "You said you could take him by yourself. Prove it."

Eeyore tugged. He almost pulled the wolf off his feet. The wolf dug his claws into the detritus covering the road. He curled his body around to snap and slash at Eeyore, but each time, the donkey danced away and tugged, grinding his big square teeth into the wolf's tail.

Their dance continued around and around. Slowly, they moved closer to the tall trees.

The little donkey's nostrils flared. His white-rimmed eyes stared at the world passing by, and his breath came hard and fast. It had been a long day. Both animals danced more slowly. The fight got quieter and more desperate. They still danced closer to the tall trees.

Eeyore thought as he fought. *What's going to happen if I manage to bite this tail off? I'm just barely keeping the wolf from me because of my hold on its tail, but I can't let go either.*

The wolf snarled, "Eventually, I'm going to rip you apart."

Eeyore would've responded with a probably, but, as his mouth had the wolf's tail in it, he couldn't. *He'll probably rip me apart.*

The watching wolves moved out of the way as the battle continued to shift farther toward them, the tall trees, and the sleeping pack leader.

Eeyore saw a big round rock and avoided it with his hooves. He also saw the pack leader lying still even as the desperate battle took place almost over him.

The little donkey felt the wolf slash his side. With his hooves planted securely, Eeyore gave a tremendous yank on the tail to pull the wolf away from his injured side.

The yank pulled the wolf away. The wolf leaped with the yank to keep from being pulled off his feet. He ended up standing over the sleeping pack leader.

One of the other wolves said, "Oh, no. Don't wake him up. Definitely, don't step on him.

The wolf fighting Eeyore snarled before he registered the warning, "The end is starting. I'll cut and slash you, until you can't fight back. I'll rip your innards out while you're still alive."

The whole threat took place as they danced some more. Eeyore desperately tried to keep the wolf from wounding him again. The wolf danced, looking for another opportunity. Somehow, he didn't step on the sleeping wolf.

Eeyore saw the wolf look down. The wolf said, "Oh, no."

The donkey looked down, too, and he saw the sleeping wolf. *Oh, no. If we wake him up, I'm going to be fighting two wolves.*

The wolf fighting Eeyore pulled against the donkey's hold on his tail. He dug his short claws into the soil and needles under the tall pine trees. One of his paws scratched needles and dust onto the pack leader's nose.

The pack leader sneezed. The fight above him stopped as the two combatants froze. Both of them looked. The pack leader lay still.

Eeyore's eyes went even wider showing a red rim around the

26

white. *We need to move away from him. This isn't going to work.*

The donkey leaned toward the lake. Eeyore pulled hard against the weight of the wolf.

The wolf pulled harder the other direction.

Eeyore felt the wolf pulling him toward the pack leader. *If I wake the other wolf, he'll help this one kill me.* Eeyore shifted. He leaned his heavy, short body toward the lake and gave a mighty tug on the tail.

That wolf let out a yelp. At first, Eeyore thought his tug had really hurt the wolf. Then, the little donkey saw the thing that had caused the terror-filled yelp. It wasn't from Eeyore's efforts.

The pack leader had awakened and lifted his head to bump into the wolf above him. The fighting wolf jumped. The sudden release of weight overbalanced Eeyore. He fell backwards toward the water. Eeyore pulled on the tail. The wolf fell with him. They tumbled together down toward the lake.

The world spun around Eeyore. All the way, he held on to the wolf's tail. Eeyore just missed the end of a broken tree leaning over the lake. A sudden tug, snap, and his teeth slammed together.

Eeyore hit the water with a big splash. Beside him came another splash. The donkey swam away. He saw the wolf swimming for the shore.

The fight must be over. How did I survive? I was lucky the wolf jumped. I was lucky we fell into the lake. Above him, none of the other wolves came to the edge of the lake. *How did that happen? I'm not lucky.*

With a sigh of relief, Eeyore swam down the lake. He spotted a place well away from the wolves with a bit of a beach to climb out of the lake. He wound stung in the cold water. *I'll probably get an infection in it and die.*

Behind him and to the side, Eeyore spotted the wolf dragging itself out of the water. The last two thirds of its tail hung straight down. *Too bad, it looks like I only almost bit it off.*

Eeyore realized he hadn't heard any thunder for a while. The dark clouds over the mountains seemed to be breaking up. *There still could be another lightning strike. If it hit me out here in the lake, I'd probably die. I better move faster.*

The donkey swam a little faster. He wasn't good at going faster, but he could've swum for a long time. *I'm getting cold. I want to get out before the sun sets.* He looked at the mountains above the lake to his left. The sun had just dropped out of sight.

The beach drew near. His front hooves struck bottom, and Eeyore climbed out and shook. Water flew away. Carefully, he climbed the steep slope. At the top, he turned to go around a tree.

Pain, another just like the previous fly bite, zapped his rump. In quick succession, things happened.

Eeyore heard the beginnings of a threat. "I'll get—"

His hind hooves lashed out and smashed into something. From the blind spot directly behind him, the wolf arced up into the air. He tumbled limply in the air and landed with a splash.

Eeyore stared at it. The wolf floated but didn't move. *I survived. I shouldn't have walked so close to the wolves. I'm sorry, Mom. I'll keep trying not to die.* The donkey turned away and plodded on. *I wonder how far I'm going to have to search for a new home. I see some buildings at the end of this lake. It's getting cold.* Eeyore shivered.

Chapter Four

Pooh and the Big Rock

Bears have a reflective layer in their eyes called the tapetum ludidum, which enhances their ability to see in low-light conditions. This reflective layer bounces light back through the retina, allowing light-sensitive cells to react a second time and greatly improving night vision.

Black bears have acute close-up vision but not good distance vision. Their hearing is twice as good as a human's. Their sense of smell is extremely good and around seven times better than a blood hound.

Pooh jumped into the dark entrance to the tunnel. He let out a howl when his head hit the ceiling. The force of his jump, hitting his head, and the slope of the tunnel caused the little black bear to tumble. Pooh bounced against the side as the tunnel made a turn.

He tumbled first one way and then another way. Pooh tried to gain control of his tumbling, but it didn't work. The little bear curled up with his paws over his head.

Finally, Pooh landed on his back and slid much more gently down the slide. He let out a sigh and lifted his head to look. The tunnel-slide stretched out into the darkness. *I hope this tunnel isn't going to hurt my shirt.* Pooh always wore his old red shirt that he loved so much.

The bottom of the slide had just a little water and felt very

29

smooth. *I wonder how the others are doing.* After thinking about it, Pooh stretched out his paws to either side and gently touched the sides of the tunnel to control his sliding.

Experimentally, Pooh pushed harder on the sides of the slide. Just as he'd guessed, his one front paw hurt. *This slide isn't scary. I don't need to slow down.*

A scream changed that thought. Pooh heard a scream echo back to him from somewhere ahead. It sounded like the young woman, Izzy.

Is it the wolf and weasel we're chasing? What's happening? Have they ambushed the others? How could they in this tunnel?

Pooh thought on the idea, trying to decide what he could do. "Oh, bother." *I can't stop. My paw hurts too much to try, and, even if I could stop, I can't help until I get there. I hope it isn't the wolf and the weasel.*

He slid past a pool of light. Rays of sunlight light shined into the tunnel from above, brightening the view. Fronds of a fern hung in front of him. Ahead, Pooh saw another pool of light. Even in the very dim light, Pooh could make out other details.

Pooh tried to think of possibilities. *I could float in here like the fish in their bubbles, but how would that help?*

The little bear remembered the promise he'd made to find the thieves and retrieve the stolen crystal. *I hope we don't have to fight.*

Pooh thought of how the pika had pushed on him with an invisible force. *If I could do that, I could slow down or go faster.*

He remembered something even more useful. Pooh remembered how he'd accidentally used lightning against the wolf. *Could I do that again?* The little bear felt a tingling on his skin. It felt similar to when he'd made lightning strike.

30

Pooh didn't want lightning to strike. He stopped thinking about it. His skin stopped tingling. Pooh sighed in relief.

What am I going to do? I don't want to fight.

Pooh thought of how the wolf named Lightning had tried to kill him. *Oh, bother. They probably won't just give the crystal back and say 'We're sorry.'* Pooh really didn't want to think about it. He'd much rather be thinking about how to get some honey. At that thought, his tummy rumbled. Pooh patted his stomach. "Yes, honey would be good."

Some more water dribbled into the tunnel, and, on the slicker slide, Pooh moved faster. Ahead of him, Pooh saw something. One small detail on the roof of the tunnel looked different. The thing shifted. Something small, only a couple of inches long, maybe three, moved on the ceiling.

The thing jumped and landed on his nose. It obviously wasn't a thing. A small, shiny animal with big eyes looked at Pooh. "Hello, may I impose on you for a ride?"

Pooh crossed his eyes trying to see the animal. With its big shiny eyes, Pooh thought it could be a small lizard. This animal's skin glistens. *Lizards have dry skin.* "What are you?"

The animal answered, "I'm a long-toed salamander. A squirrel came down. He looked too small to ride with. A dog-wolf came past. She seemed to be enjoying herself, but I didn't trust her. A human came past, but she screamed when she saw me. I don't think it would've worked to jump on her."

Pooh said, "No. I don't think it would've worked for you to jump onto Izzy. The dog's name is Annie. She isn't a wolf, and she would've been nice to you. Why did you think I was safe?"

"You had a relaxed, contemplative attitude about you. I thought you would talk first and eat me later. That is, if you would try to eat me."

31

"Do you think I'm going to try to eat you?"

"No, I think you're safe. Why are you going down the slide?"

"I made some new friends today. They had something important stolen. We're chasing after the thieves. A wolf and a weasel stole a crystal."

While they talked, Pooh continued sliding down the tunnel. More rays of sunlight broke through the dark to brighten the tunnel. A small bump in the slide jostled Pooh. "I think this ride might get bumpy. You better hold on."

The little bear hit another bump. It didn't hurt, but the bump made Pooh lose contact with the bottom of the slide. The little salamander lifted off the bear's nose. He just held on with his front toes.

"That was good advice."

They came back down, and the salamander flattened himself on Pooh's nose. The little bear felt the smallest pressure from the creatures toes as it held on.

They hit another bump and went airborne. This time, the salamander didn't have any trouble hanging on.

Unfortunately, Pooh came down poorly. He hit another bump and tumbled head over heels. Pooh protectively held his paws over the little creature on his nose.

With a *whump*, Pooh landed on his back. The air was knocked out of him. The little bear gasped. *Oh, my. That wasn't fun.*

The salamander said, "That was quite a ride. Too bad we can't go back and do it again."

Pooh nodded his head. "I wouldn't want to, but I'm glad you enjoyed it."

The salamander asked, "What did you say about thieves and trying to get something back?"

"We are after a wolf and a weasel. They stole a crystal."

The salamander said, "That seems crazy. I've never heard of an important crystal, and I've seen crystals my whole life."

Pooh didn't know what to think or say. *Why would a crystal be important?* "I haven't heard of an important crystal before. I don't know why this one's important. The squirrel had it."

The salamander asked, "What was the squirrel doing with it?"

The tunnel had dropped just a little. Pooh didn't answer. He concentrated on keeping his head steady. They went into a sharp turn, and, together, they slid part way up the side as they went through the curve. Pooh said, "I'm a little clumsy. I hope I don't start tumbling again."

"I'll be okay. I can move very fast."

Pooh slid back to the bottom. He remembered the unanswered question. "The squirrel was supposed to keep the crystal safe. He's quite upset at having it stolen." After a moment Pooh added, "The squirrel is a secret agent."

The little salamander asked, "What's a secret agent?"

"I don't know."

The little salamander said, "I don't want to sound discouraging, but I can't see you or the others taking on a wolf and a weasel."

Pooh said, "You could be right. I guess we're doing it because it's the right thing to do, but it might not be smart. I should talk with the others about our goal. That would be smart."

The salamander didn't answer. Pooh stopped trying to look it. Looking cross-eyed had made his head start hurting. Curiously, the little bear watched the roof of the wall go past. Every now and then, the roof disappeared and he could see the sky. Tree branches flew by above him, and bushes hung over the edge of the slide.

The view disappeared as they slid back into darkness. The slide leveled out, and they slowed. Ahead, more light brightened the view. Pooh smelled a different type of dampness. It made him think of one of the moist meadows.

The salamander must've recognized the smell. "Could you lift your head a bit?"

Pooh lifted his nose toward the ceiling. A cool breeze blew in from the opening just ahead.

The salamander said, "Thank you for the ride." It jumped off Pooh's nose and landed on a fern growing beside the slide.

As Pooh slid away, he heard the salamander say one more thing, "Good luck on your foolish quest."

The words bothered the little bear. Pooh hadn't heard any more screams from Izzy. *She was afraid of a little salamander. How will she react to a wolf?*

Pooh remembered the last words he'd heard from the wolf. *Next time, we'll have another pack with us. We'll have too many for this bear to deal with. He'll be like the last victim you ran from.*

The little bear didn't like that memory. There wouldn't be just one wolf. *I don't like how this story is going. I don't want so much danger in my story.* The poor little bear also wanted to help his friends. Another scream came from ahead.

What will it be this time? Did a mouse or a little snake frighten her? Pooh decided that Izzy would be so frightened by the wolves that she might not even scream.

Pooh tried not to think about the wolves any more. The slide

34

helped. One moment, he slid along slowly, looking out at another small meadow, and, the next moment, water, cold water, poured over the side.

The cold of the water surprised him. A sudden drop through the air to a small swirling pool followed by a drop into another section of the tunnel convinced him that Izzy must've screamed at that experience.

The tunnel and slide steepened. Pooh picked up speed. He tried to slow down using his paws. Trying hurt his one troublesome sore paw, and it didn't help.

The slide swerved around in big long curves. Instead of going slower, Pooh slid faster. His speed and the water running with him pushed him high up on to the side.

Down he went into another big turn. Pooh swept up high on the other side. This continued, with the little bear going higher and higher with each succeeding curve.

Pooh heard Izzy scream again. This time the scream seemed different, almost as if it got cut off before she finished. This third scream left the bear puzzled. *Is there any warning or need for help in her screams? This one seemed different. She could just be frightened by a bug, but her scream cut off.*

He flew up into another curve. This time, Pooh soared up and flipped upside down. His thoughts evaporated. A wail burst from his mouth. "AAAAAAH!"

Pooh continued on, zooming through curves, sliding upside down, and swooshing through the tunnel. Pooh opened his mouth and let his tongue hang out.

His speed slowed, but the sides of the slide still sped by. Pooh's thoughts returned. *That was fun. I was afraid at first, but I've never done something like this before. Izzy just screamed about that last section. There's nothing to worry about. I think the salamander was right. It would be fun to do this again.*

Pooh wondered what Izzy would scream about next. *She'll probably scream at the bottom when we drop into the pool of water.*

Far ahead, light glimmered. In the light, Pooh could see clearly. Eagerly, he looked ahead. He could see a long way. *This section is very straight.* Something just past the light didn't look right.

The tunnel usually had a certain look to it. With light, the walls sometimes glistened like the salamander did. The center of the tunnel had looked darker unless light shined off the wall of a bend in the tunnel. Pooh squinted, trying to make out what he saw. It almost looked like—

Pooh saw a reflection far ahead. The reflection filled the middle of the tunnel. It didn't seem to be a bend.

The little bear let out a wail. "Aaaah."

The little bear jammed his paws against the side of the slide in a frantic effort to stop. *I'm not slowing fast enough.*

I don't see Annie or Izzy. How did they survive this? Pooh pushed his paws as hard as he could against the slick side. He ignored the pain. *What happened to the others?*

Pooh still sped down the tunnel. He had no way to stop. Pooh couldn't stop in time. Ahead of him, the light revealed a boulder. The boulder blocked the way.

Chapter Five

A Surprise Ally

In one sense, gravity is very simple. Objects with more mass have more gravity. The farther you are from an object, the less you feel its gravity. These things we know, but we do not know how gravitational force is transmitted. Some theories postulate a hypothetical particle called the graviton. That particle transmits gravity. In Einstein's theory, gravity isn't transmitted but rather is a consequence of the curvature of space time caused by mass and energy. That is mind-stretching stuff, and here is more and very exciting mind-stretching stuff. Imagine what you could do if you could control gravity.

Pooh's claws scratched against the smooth walls of the tunnel as he frantically tried to stop. In the area of light, Pooh could see the boulder all too well. *I'm going to hit it.* He let out a wail, "Aaah." His last thought was about Izzy's third scream. *This time it had been bad.* Pooh wailed again.

His stomach lurched, and Pooh brushed past some bushes and tumbled to an upside down stop. He heard the sound of a stream. *What just happened?* Tall straight trees grew around the area, and P'Nut jumped toward Pooh. P'Nut turned his head upside down to look at Pooh. "Are you okay?"

The big newfie dog, Annie, sat on the ground by the young woman, Izzy. The dog asked, "Are you okay? I hope I didn't hurt you."

Pooh said, "I think so, but I haven't tried moving yet. Did you save me?"

Annie said, "I was afraid to use my ability to control gravity."

Pooh asked, "Why? You can do amazing things with it."

Annie said, "Yes, but I drowned Izzy. If Coyote hadn't saved her, she'd be dead."

Izzy said, "But I didn't die. I'm okay."

P'Nut interrupted. "Okay, okay. That's all good, but we have a problem. That boulder was knocked into the slide. We should let the others up by Aneroid lake know. If someone comes down, they could get hurt. Plus, I've smelled around."

Pooh noticed a familiar smell. "It was the wolf. Wasn't it?" Pooh smelled carefully. It didn't quite smell like the wolf called Lightning.

P'Nut had been shifting back and forth. He said, "Yes. Yes. I found where the wolf dug dirt away to cause the boulder to roll into the slide."

Annie said, "If only Fuego was still with us, he would be able to fly back and warn them."

Izzy said, "From what those other hummingbirds said, I don't think our hummingbird friend survived."

Pooh rolled over and scratched his head in thought. "Annie, you used your ability to control gravity to yank me out of the slide. Why don't you just use that same ability to yank the boulder out of the slide?"

Annie said, "Everything happened so quickly. I didn't want to hurt anyone again. I didn't want to be a bad dog. I'm sorry."

Pooh answered, "It's okay, Annie. I have trouble thinking when events move too fast, but now, you could just lift the boulder out of the way and remove the danger for anyone using the slide."

P'Nut said, "Annie, you should lift the boulder out of the slide."

Annie said, "Okay."

The boulder lifted up into the air along with smaller rocks and some globules of water. The floating objects moved away from the group and weaved in-between the tall trees. At a safe distance from the slide, they fell to the ground with a crashes and splashes.

P'Nut said, "Okay, okay. That's done. We have to get moving. We don't know where the wolf and the weasel went. Their smell seems old. I don't think they're near here. We need to follow their scent."

Pooh stood on his hind paws and pointed a paw down the stream. "From what I smell, they went that way." *That's the direction to the wolf or wolves.* A shudder ran down Pooh's back.

P'Nut said, "I agree. Let's go. Let's go."

The little squirrel didn't wait for anyone else to say anything. He started running and hopping over the ground.

Izzy said, "Remember what the beaver said about the possibilities of flash floods."

Pooh turned his head. Had he seen something? A breeze blew through the tall pine trees around them. The leaves on other thin trees, really more bushes than trees, shivered. Pooh lifted his nose into the breeze. His senses told him of something wrong, very wrong. "Oh bother." *What's wrong? I'm trying to find a wolf and probably more wolves. That's what's wrong.*

He heard the sound his own paws made in the needles carpeting the forest floor. Pine needles and pinecones littered every open part of the forest floor around them.

Pooh twitched his ears back and forth, trying to catch any notice of danger. He heard the sounds of his friends walking.

His nose told him of a number of edible plants. Pooh wanted to follow those smells. It wouldn't take him long to find the plants. He'd seen some by the little stream and suspected more of the plants grew here. Pooh's stomach rumbled. A few unusual smells mixed in. One grew stronger. *What's that?* It stood out from the normal plants and animals. Pooh also smelled the dry dustiness. The little bear sneezed.

I don't smell very many other animals. Where is everyone? When I came here with my dad, he said that this area by the lake is a dangerous area. Oh, I don't like this story. "Do we really need to get this crystal?"

P'Nut said, "Yes. Move faster."

Pooh walked on two paws just like humans walked on two feet. Long ago, he'd injured one of his front paws, and it hurt to walk on it. After the very long day, Pooh's hind paws didn't feel much better.

P'Nut rapidly got ahead. The bear looked back for Annie and Izzy. They moved even more slowly. *We aren't ready to face one wolf, let alone two packs.* Pooh followed after P'Nut and carefully smelled the air. He trusted his nose. His eyes couldn't see very far. The little bear thought he smelled deer. *They wouldn't be around if the wolf is around.* "Deer, I can smell you. We are chasing after a wolf and a weasel. They are bad. Did you see them?"

Silence followed Pooh's question.

P'Nut jumped onto one of the trees. He said, "I can see you over there. I see you. Please, just answer the question."

More silence and then a voice answered, "We saw them. They ran down by the road. The wolf fell. A robot took the wolf. I don't know what happened to the weasel. You should leave. Do not come back."

Another one of the deer argued, "No. They should stay."

The words stopped Pooh. He remembered his father warning him about a strange person in control of the lodge by the lake. He'd also said something about robots. He'd been frightened of the wolves, but robots were worse. Pooh knew that a wolf would be dangerous, but a robot had killed the wolf. The robot had to be more dangerous. The strange odor had grown stronger. *Is that the robot?*

The bear looked at his friends. "I thought we could maybe get the crystal back from one wolf, but robots are worse. You just heard what happened to the wolf. What should we do?"

Izzy stooped to pick up some rocks. "We need to keep going, but we should be prepared."

Keep going? This is crazy. Pooh asked, "What are the rocks for?"

"I can throw a rock very fast and very accurately."

P'Nut said, "Oh, oh, that's good. Let's go."

Pooh looked back at the squirrel. *They're both crazy.* P'Nut ran and hopped over the ground. Pooh's ears told him Annie and Izzy had started walking again. Without thinking about it, Pooh started walking. *I don't like this story. It's too scary.* He argued with himself. *I need to help my friends. Izzy has a good idea. I'm glad she can do something helpful. What can I do? Could I do lightning again?* Pooh tried to remember how he'd done it before, but he wasn't sure if he could do it again.

Izzy asked, "Pooh, why are you walking back up the mountain?"

Pooh looked around. He stood right in front of Annie and Izzy. They were going the wrong way. *Wait.* "I think my paws had their own idea of which way to go." Reluctantly, he turned around and resumed walking downhill.

Annie asked, "I wonder why the wolf and weasel came here. Is their home by this lake?"

P'Nut said, "No, no. The wolf was helping the weasel. The weasel is trying to get the crystal to some bad people. We have to get the crystal from this robot and get it to Noah."

41

Pooh stopped. "P'Nut, how do you know all of this?"

P'Nut looked back and shook his tail. "I was just an ordinary squirrel, but I had an adventure and met someone or a thing called Mr. Bond. He told me about Annie and this crystal. I volunteered to help get both Annie and the crystal to safety. Bond communicates to me with this gadget." He tapped a small device on his suit. "He sent me that gadget I used to help save you from the bad man. Bond's enemies have figured out what he's doing and are causing trouble. We need to find the crystal. Now, I'm a secret agent."

Pooh wondered what a secret agent was. He asked, "Can this Bond help us?"

"Bond isn't able to communicate with me right now, but I hope he can help. Come on. Come on" The squirrel turned and raced ahead.

Izzy pushed on Pooh's back. "Come on, Pooh. I'd like to stop and rest, but we better go. This crazy squirrel might get into trouble."

Ahead of them, through the trees, Pooh saw the road. It was a straight path with weeds and grasses growing on it. Pooh remembered riding up that road with his dad just that morning. So much had happened since then. *Robots? I hope Dad made it home safely. Was it really only this morning he brought me up here?*

P'Nut's voice came back to Pooh and the others. "Something isn't right up here. I smell something strange."

Pooh said, "Wait for us. I smell something strange, too. Maybe it's the robot." He tried to speed up, but the long day had definitely caught up with him. Pooh just limped along.

A glimpse of some white caught his attention. His nose verified. Snowberries grew in tight bushy stands. Pooh's stomach grumbled. He could eat some, but the effort of just walking to them seemed too much. Also, he sensed danger.

Under the tall trees, the light of dusk was very dim. Pooh looked around. He listened for any warnings of danger. His nose already wasn't happy with the smells, other than the edible food smells. Pooh wanted to know what was happening. *This is too scary.*

From behind, Pooh heard Izzy. "P'Nut, we've had a very hard and long day. We need to stop and rest."

Pooh agreed. He limped on. The pinecones scattered on the ground didn't help. Ahead, he saw the hyperactive squirrel running around and sniffing at the ground.

P'Nut said, "I think the wolf fell here. There's a faint odor in the air but no scent trail on the ground. I can smell something strange. This must be where the deer saw the robot take the wolf. The weasel ran through the tall grass over here."

Pooh also smelled something else. The bear lifted his nose higher. There it was. He smelled a deer. *Is a deer following us? Why would it do that?*

The squirrel moved out of sight Pooh yelled after him, "P'Nut, wait up. We don't want to get separated."

P'Nut jumped out of the grass and landed on a tree. "Then, hurry up. You guys are taking forever."

Annie said, "Go on ahead, Pooh. Izzy and I'll catch up. Go help P'Nut figure out what happened."

A bird flew past. Another flew up and landed on a branch above them.

Pooh wanted to cry. *I can't go any faster. Is my dad okay?* Pooh tried to go faster. Instead, he stumbled on a pinecone and fell. He landed face down but rolled to his back. Pooh wanted to stay on his back. It felt good to rest.

P'Nut yelled, "The weasel is close. I can smell it."

Pooh sighed and mumbled to himself, "Oh, bother." With an effort, he struggled back onto his hind paws. *This story is not good.*

P'Nut stood, looking into a bush. His tail waved back and forth over his back. "Come out, Weasel."

A scratchy voice spoke, "About time you found me. Are you missing something?"

P'Nut spoke in a very angry voice. "Yes, yes, you thief. Give it back. Give it back, or I'll make you give it back."

"You and what army? There's only one of me, but I can still beat you very easily."

At that moment, Pooh finally caught up. The little bear recognized the round, little red things on the bush. *This is a rose bush.* Pooh leaned over, trying to catch his breath and spot the weasel. *I don't like that voice. It sounds nasty.*

P'Nut jumped back and forth. "I'll come in after you."

"Oh, look. It looks like a baby bear came to help you. I'm so scared. Not."

It had been a very long day for Pooh. All of his paws hurt. He was hungry. He was tired. He was worried about his dad. His stomach was not happy about giving away the honey. The comment about him being a baby was the last straw.

Pooh remembered scaring the wolves with lightning. He remembered how it felt to do it. His fur lifted. Pooh thrust a paw out in the voice's direction. "I'm not a baby. I may be a small bear, but I'm too big to sit in peoples' laps anymore. I'm almost one hundred pounds. How does this feel?"

Pooh tried to aim what he hoped was the lightning strike. A flash of light and a small boom followed. Disappointingly for Pooh, it didn't seem nearly as strong a lightning strike as the one he'd fixed on the wolf.

The weasel let out a yell, "Oww, stop. I'm coming out. No need to get nasty. I don't have the crystal, but I know who took it."

A small creature, as long as P'Nut's body, slunk out of the bush. It had chestnut brown fur on the top half of its body and a lighter cream color on the lower half.

Izzy must've gotten closer because she spoke from right behind Pooh. "Oh, you're such a cute little guy."

The weasel said, in a much nicer voice, "You have a woman with you."

It ran past Pooh. The bear turned around to see Izzy lean down. The little weasel scampered onto her outstretched hand. "Ah, this is better. With this lady's help, we might be able to get the crystal back."

Pooh had a bad feeling about the whereabouts of the crystal.

P'Nut asked, "Where's the crystal?"

"When the creature took the wolf, he also took the crystal. He loaded the wolf into the back of a vehicle and drove down the road."

P'Nut said, "Let's go after it."

Annie said, "It is getting dark. The rest of us are very tired. I think we should find somewhere to spend the night."

Pooh munched on a couple of the red rose hips hanging on the bush. He looked around. Pooh hadn't noticed how dark it was getting. He lifted his nose to smell. He smelled the vehicle. Pooh also smelled the strange out-of-place odor. It had grown stronger. It must be the robot. The deer smell had grown fainter. *The deer must've moved on.*

Pooh thought he saw something move. It came closer.

Chapter Six

The Cabin

Years ago, I thought of how possibly in a distant future scientists could learn how to turn quantum effects into macro effects. I decided to use that idea in my books. Just two weeks later, I stumbled across a scientific study proposing laying the groundwork to turn quantum effects into macro effects. Some quantum effects have already been turned into macro effects. Crazy, right? P'Nut's vibrating is borrowing from a quantum effect called tunneling.

Just imagine if you could jump through a door or a wall.

Pooh said, "I think someone's coming up the road."

P'Nut jumped up on a pole. "It's a human. I think a young woman or girl."

Pooh sighed in relief.

P'Nut said, "Let's go talk to her."

The squirrel didn't wait for a response. He jumped off the pole and ran up the road.

Izzy said, "Wait up, P'Nut."

Annie said, "Let's go."

Pooh watched Izzy and Annie follow P'Nut. *Somehow, I've ended up sitting on the ground. It feels good to rest.*

Izzy called back, "Are you coming, Pooh?"

Oh, bother. They might need my help. The little bear struggled up onto his hind paws and limped after them.

A bird silently sailed past in-between them.

The person on the road called out, "Who are you?"

P'Nut answered, "We are travelers, looking for somewhere to stay the night. I'm P'Nut."

Pooh stopped and scratched his head. *Why didn't he tell her why we are here? She might know something.*

Izzy said, "We heard from some deer that a wolf got taken by a robot. That sounds dangerous."

The person looked around. "It is dangerous. You should leave early tomorrow."

P'Nut dashed about on the road and, then, sat on his haunches. "No robot is going to get me. I'm too fast, but some of my friends are worried about the robot. Do you know anything about it?"

Pooh had gotten close enough to tell it was a tall, skinny girl talking to them.

The girl looked around again before responding, I... I don't know."

To Pooh, she looked nervous. He said, "Thanks for the warning. Do you know of any shelter, maybe an abandoned building we could use for the night?"

"Come with me. I'll show you a cabin that should work. There are many abandoned buildings up here. No one wants to live around here anymore. Be sure to leave very early in the morning. Don't go any closer to the lake."

The girl turned around and started walking down the middle of the road. On both sides, dark trees crowded the edge of the road. The first stars of the evening glimmered over the road.

In the quiet of the night, Pooh heard the murmuring sounds of the nearby river. He remembered the river from when his foster father brought him up to the trail.

Izzy asked, "Why do you live here?"

The girl didn't answer. She just kept walking. Pooh saw how she walked with her head bowed and shoulders squeezed in. *I've never known anyone that looked like her. I think something is wrong. Maybe Izzy will have an idea. She's a human and might understand.* He walked after the girl with everyone else. Luckily, because of his sore paws and how tired he was, they didn't have to go very far.

She pointed to their left. Back from the road stood a house. Dark, spooky trees stood silently around them in the darkening evening.

The girl said, "Go right on in. The door won't be locked."

Pooh turned his head in surprise and concern. The murmuring sounds of the river had grown stronger. It roared. "What's happening?"

The girl said, "There's a flash flood down in the river. You're high enough up here to be safe. The flooding will be much worse by the lake. That might give you more time to leave in the morning. Still, leave first thing in the morning."

Pooh heard her words, but he kept listening to the river.

P'Nut asked, "What do you think of this cabin, Izzy?"

"I think we should go in. I need to empty my backpack and lay out my sleeping bag. Some of my things got wet going down the slide. I hope my sleeping bag stayed dry. We can look for food." She looked

48

at Pooh and the weasel. "I have some food for Annie and me, but not much. I don't know if you can eat any of it."

The weasel said, "Put me down. There are mice and rats around. I'll find my own food. I'll see you in the morning. We can figure out a plan."

Izzy lowered the hand carrying it, and the weasel jumped to the ground and scampered off into the grass and weeds.

Pooh said, "I've been browsing all day, but I could use some more food. Do you have any honey?"

Izzy laughed, "No, Pooh. I'm sorry. I don't have any honey. Maybe we'll find some in the house."

P'Nut scampered up the driveway toward the old house. "Come on."

Everyone followed, including Pooh. He also looked around. The grass looked dry and not very appetizing. He didn't see any other plants that looked better. His stomach rumbled. Pooh patted it. *I know. This doesn't look good, but we're with friends. They need our help.*

Just before he reached the house, Pooh smelled something promising. *I'll come back out here later.*

Standing on the porch, P'Nut looked back at them from the house. The squirrel twitched his tail every now and then. Izzy walked up the steps and looked in a window. Annie walked up and started smelling around the house. There was a metal bucket with spots of rust in the corner of the porch.

Above them, Pooh heard a gentle breeze blowing through the pine needles. He walked up and asked, "Are we going in?"

Izzy said, "I can't see anything through the window."

Annie said, "No one has been here for a long time. I can't smell

49

any fresh smells. There are some older animal smells. A few fresher rodent smells, but it does seem abandoned."

P'Nut said, "I would open the door, but I'm a bit too small." He looked around at the hesitant group and said, "I guess I'll just have to break the door down."

Pooh stared at the little squirrel in surprise.

Izzy just had time to ask, "What?"

The little squirrel ran at the door and jumped. He disappeared through it.

Izzy gasped in surprise. "What just happened?"

Through the door, Pooh heard P'Nut say, "It's a bit darker in here and dusty, but there isn't anything to be worried about."

Pooh thought about what had just happened. *How did P'Nut do that?* Pooh stepped up to the door and reached out a paw. The paw didn't go through the door. Instead, his paw pushed against the door. At first, it didn't open. Pooh leaned his almost-one-hundred-pound cub's body against the door. With a creak of complaint, the door opened.

The inside did seem darker. It took Pooh just a second for his eyes to adjust to the darker interior. P'Nut stood in front of the doorway. Vaguely, Pooh made out furniture.

P'Nut said, "Thanks for opening the door. It gives me a bit more light to see with, but I still can't see well in here. We need a light."

Pooh asked, "How did you go through the door?"

P'Nut answered, "I don't know how I do it, but I know how to make it happen. When I go through things, it feels like I'm vibrating."

Pooh walked around the little squirrel and started to explore. "I can see things, but it's a bit dark."

50

P'Nut said, "I'm going back outside and look for food."

Izzy asked, "Pooh, what can you see? Do you know what candles are?"

Pooh answered, "The couple who raised me had me inside more when I was very little. I remember they used candles in the evening. There's a fireplace and a shelf above it with candles."

Izzy said, "Pooh, it's too dark in here for me to see. Can you help me get to the candles?"

Pooh turned around to see the young woman standing just inside the door. Annie walked around her and started smelling the room.

The little bear walked to Izzy and said, "Here, hold my paw."

He gently touched one of her hands with a paw. Izzy grabbed it and said, "Okay, lead me to the candles. I can light them."

Pooh carefully led her around a chair and past another type of furniture. The little bear wasn't sure what it was. He stopped below the shelf with the candles. "We are just below the shelf. Izzy, lift your hand. I'll tell you which way to move it."

The little bear watched Izzy lifting her other hand up. "The shelf is a little higher."

"I found the shelf."

Pooh pulled on the paw she held. "Move your hand this way. The candles are close."

Izzy held her hand open. Slowly, she moved it until it bumped against a candle.

Pooh heard the success and happiness in her voice as she said, "I've got it."

Izzy let go of his paw and sat on the floor. "Pooh, can you scoot my backpack closer to me?"

The little bear walked to her backpack and scooted it right up to her.

"Thanks. In a minute, I'll get us some light. Then, I can explore."

Pooh left her to her candle. He started exploring by himself. Old, old smells led him to the kitchen. He sniffed around, and his stomach rumbled in hope. The drawers were all pulled out, and the cupboard doors hung wide open. He couldn't see for sure, but the cupboards looked bare.

Annie came up to him and said, "There is something in here I don't recognize."

Things were scattered about the floor. Pooh walked carefully through the mess.

Pooh lifted his nose and sniffed the air. There was something different. He'd been looking for anything edible, in particular, honey. He had noticed an odd smell and hadn't thought anything of it. Now, though, he followed Annie and the odor back out of the kitchen and down a hall. The hall had open cupboards and things on the floor. Pooh felt a gentle movement of air and noticed the broken glass. "There's a window broken back here."

From behind him, flickering light started coming closer. It lit up the sharp shards of glass littering the floor. A very large pot cast a flickering shadow on the wall behind it. "What's that doing in here?"

Annie spoke from another room. "The smell's stronger in here."

Izzy walked up with her candle. "What are you two looking for?"

Annie said, "We've been following a strange smell. It's stronger in this room."

Izzy and Pooh entered the room. Light filled the room. This room also had stuff scattered on the floor. Something fluttered.

Izzy screamed.

The scream startled Pooh, and he backed out of the room, tripped, and landed headfirst in the pot. He tumbled over with the pot over his head. The pot muffled the noises around him, but he could make out what was being said.

Izzy said, "I'm sorry for screaming. You startled me."

Annie said, "Oh, it's a bat. Hello, how are you? Would you like to be our friend?"

Pooh managed to get his front paws on the pot. He pushed. The pot didn't move. "Oh, bother." His whispered words echoed in the pot.

The bat answered, "Who are you? Why are you here? Do you know of the danger?"

Izzy said, "I'm Izzy. These are my friends. We are after something important that was stolen. What danger do you know of?"

"I have flown in many places. This place is haunted. There are few animals. At night, when I hunt, I hear cries of pain and fear. I need to hunt."

"Where are the voices coming from?"

Annie said, "I don't think he heard your question before he left."

Izzy asked, "Where's Pooh?"

The little bear wriggled, making all the noise he could. "I'm stuck in this pot. Help."

Annie said, "He was right here. Wait. Did you hear that noise?"

Pooh called, "Help."

Izzy said, "It's coming from the hall."

Relief flowed through Pooh as he heard Izzy's footsteps draw near.

"You silly old bear, how did you get your head stuck in that pot? Did it have honey in it?"

Pooh sniffed and sneezed. He didn't smell any honey, just dust. "No honey. I tripped."

Izzy said, "That looks stuck on him. I'll go out and get the bucket on the porch. With it, I'll get some water. We'll use the water to wet the edges of the pot around Pooh's neck. That should help get it off him."

Pooh heard her walk away. *I think I'll try again.* This time the little bear got all four paws on the rim of the pot. He pushed, wriggled, and twisted. He remained stuck. *If only this pot really had honey in it.* His stomach rumbled at the thought. The power of the thought pulled his tongue out to taste. *Yuck. Dust tastes terrible.*

The little bear sat. The heavy pot hung and pulled his head down. *I hope Izzy hurries. Much of this and my neck's going to get sore.*

Time crawled past. Pooh wondered if morning had come. A voice startled him. The little bear found himself lying on his side. Something warm lay against him.

Izzy said, "How's our silly, old bear doing?"

Annie answered, "I think we both fell asleep."

Izzy said, "Pooh, sit up and rest the pot on the floor."

Pooh rolled over. He sat up and leaned his head down, until he felt the pot hit the floor.

Izzy said, "I'll just pour some of this water around the edges until I get it good and wet."

Pooh felt water trickling around his neck and heard it splashing

54

into the bottom of the pot. He sighed. *This is good. They'll have me out in no time at all.* Pooh twisted his head to help spread the water into his fur and around the pot.

A splash of water got his nose wet. His nose wasn't just getting splashed. The water had filled the bottom of the pot. He snorted water. "Help, I'm drowning."

The poor bear struggled to breathe. He snorted water up his nose and splashed it into his eyes. He coughed. He heard Annie and Izzy trying to calm him.

"It's just a little water."

Annie said, "You'll be fine. I'm going to pull on your tail. Izzy will pull on the pot."

"PULL ON MY TAIL?"

Pooh jumped to his paws and ran. He bounced off the walls. His friends hollered, "Stop, Pooh. You're going to run into something and hurt yourself."

He stumbled on something but managed to keep on his paws.

P'Nut asked, "Did you start playing a game while I was gone?"

Izzy said, "This isn't a game."

Annie yelled, "Look out!"

Pooh heard a crash and ran into a wall at the same time. He fell back onto the floor. He blinked and sat up. Pooh shook the dust and pieces of pot out of his fur. "That's how you get a pot off your head and not by having your tail pulled."

Chapter Seven

Chance Saves Eeyore Again

Donkeys have excellent night vision. This is because of the higher abundance of rod cells in their eyes and the presence of a tapetum lucidum. They don't see red, but see red as a strange hue of green.

Albert Einstein said, "God does not play dice with the universe." Einstein believed the universe works according to strict deterministic laws. He believed the universe didn't work by chance and definitely without random possibilities, but quantum physics doesn't work the way he wanted it to.

Eeyore plodded along the road. The buildings drew nearer. To get to them, Eeyore would have to go through some trees. They were the first buildings he had seen all day, and he didn't want to lose them. *I need a new home.* The buildings stood at the edge of the lake and had what looked like an open field behind them. *This could be perfect, but something will probably go wrong.*

If I continue along this road, the trees will block my view of those buildings. I probably won't figure out how to get to the buildings for a very long time. I'm used to my pasture. I think I would get lost in the trees.

The shore had been just below the road, but now it angled off, going straight away from him toward the buildings. Carefully, in the dimming light of dusk, Eeyore made his way down to the lake. By slightly moving his head, he could see each of his hooves and carefully choose where to step.

A sound caught his attention, and Eeyore turned his ears, trying to identify the source. He'd never heard this type of sound before. It didn't end. The noise rose and fell almost like a wind blowing through trees.

Going farther along the shore, Eeyore recognized the sound as a sound of splashing. *Moving water? What's this?* The little donkey tried to remember if he'd ever seen this before. *Water ran off the roof and down onto the ground. Water must be running from up in the mountains down to here.*

The sound of the moving water grew louder. In front of him, light glimmered off a moving surface. Eeyore looked up. Stars glimmered in the night sky. The tops of the trees in front of him glowed in a very faint light. The hill and mountains behind them glowed, too. *Must be the Moon coming up behind me.*

Eeyore stepped out from the safety of the bank and into the edge of the moving water. His hoof found footing in rocks. One hoof at a time, Eeyore stepped in deeper and deeper. It felt even colder than the lake. The water kept getting deeper. The intense cold traveled up his legs. Eeyore shivered, uncontrollably, and turned around. One hoof at a time, he plodded his way back to warmth and the safety of dry land.

Eeyore looked back at the moving water. This time, he noticed something else. The bubbles that looked like balls of water carrying those green creatures moved in the air above the water. They all steadily moved upstream. *What are they doing? This world is strange. There's only one thing for me to do. I need to go up along this moving water until I find a new home or a way to cross the moving water. Then, I could go to those buildings I saw.*

The donkey plodded along the edge of the moving water. At times, he found an easy path. At other places, he had to detour around massive trees, fallen trees, logs resting against trees, boulders, or bushes. Eeyore kept going. The trees closest to the moving water had lots of sticks, branches, and the occasional log piled up on one side of them. Eeyore stared at the piles of sticks and branches. *How did they get there?*

His ears twitched. They turned back and forth. A noise caught his attention. *I could go investigate the noise, but I'd probably get lost. I better stay by this moving water.* Eeyore continued, but the noise grew louder and more varied. *I don't like those sounds.* He recognized most of the sounds as voices. He recognized pain, terror, anger, and other emotions in the voices. They sounded like trouble. *I could go investigate, but I'd end up in trouble.*

Back in the trees, a sensor lit up. With a whirr, a device turned toward Eeyore. The donkey moved behind some trees and out of view, but not before the sensor relayed its information.

The sounds grew quieter the farther up the moving water Eeyore plodded. It proved harder to forget them. He lifted his head and looked back. Through the trees and bushes, Eeyore saw a flickering light.

Eeyore turned away from the light and the memory of the sounds. *I couldn't do anything anyway.* He stood still. His head swayed back toward the flickering light. In the direction Eeyore had been going, he spotted a structure spanning the water. *I can get to those buildings by the lake.* The sounds of the moving water seemed to be different, louder. Eeyore shrugged and plodded on toward the structure.

A boulder blocked his way. *It would be shorter and easier to wade into the edge of the moving water and go around it. The other direction means climbing up higher on the bank. That won't be easy.* Eeyore took a couple of steps into the water. *That's funny. The water seems to be getting deeper.* Something flew over the water and into the trees behind him. It distracted him from continuing deeper into the stream. It also distracted him from the increasing noise of the moving water.

Eeyore stopped and looked after the object. *Whatever it is probably isn't good news.* He shivered. *It's getting colder.* Eeyore looked at his legs. The water crept higher up his legs as he looked. *I don't like this cold water. I think I'll go see if that flying thing is in the trees.*

Eeyore turned around. He waded out of the water. He watched each hoof as he climbed the bank. It took a lot of effort to climb the steep incline. Halfway up, he looked back. *Maybe I should go back. This is too hard.* A roaring sound made him look up at the structure spanning the moving water. Under it, he saw a churning mass of water and trees roaring down on him.

I'm going to drown. I told Mom I wouldn't give up. Eeyore thrust hard and jumped and jumped. With each jump Eeyore gained ground, but he also slid back some. The ground shook under him. *This is a useless battle. I'm not getting away.*

The end of a tree swept at him as it barreled along with the mass of churning water. Eeyore ducked. It missed him.

The water rose up around his hooves. The little donkey fought back. Eeyore jumped up and out of the rising water.

A roar all around Eeyore threatened to deafen him. He jumped again. He bucked against the water that threatened to pull him back.

Another wave of water and debris higher than the last rumbled and roared at him. *I can't get away.* Eeyore waded through the rising water and pushed up against a huge tree.

The flood rushed past on both sides. The water rose higher. Eeyore lifted his head to keep it out of the water. Trees floated by. His eyes went under water. Eeyore heard rocks rumbling past in the torrent. The little donkey tipped his head to keep his nose out of the water.

The water rushed past Eeyore. Waves threatened to drown him. The little donkey pawed with his front hooves against the massive trunk. Eeyore lifted his nose higher.

The water seemed to rush by Eeyore forever. He couldn't hear anything. Eeyore trembled and leaned against the tree. *This massive trunk is saving me. I'm going to be okay, but I'll probably get a cold from this freezing water and die.*

The ground continued to shudder. Only the tree stood solid. The water level dropped. Eeyore gladly stopped straining to hold his nose higher. The water fell below his eyes.

Gratefully, Eeyore leaned against the massive tree. *Thank you for saving me.* Then, the little donkey felt something big hit the tree.

Eeyore heard the tree groan. He heard a snap. He felt the tree shudder. The trunk pushed back against his small frame. The ground under his hooves shifted. It tipped. Eeyore felt the tree move. *This is it. The cold of this water is killing me. This tree is going to fall over on me and crush me. Then, the water will drown me. Then, the other trees and rocks will bury me. I'll suffocate. I think I'm going to die.*

Eeyore braced his hooves and shoved against the huge tree with all thirty inches of his might. The little donkey didn't stop shoving. The water rose again. Eeyore heard nothing, but he felt the roaring, thumping, and groaning.

Stubbornly, Eeyore kept pushing. *When will the end come? When will the tree break and crush me?* The little donkey held his place, straining with all his strength.

A voice spoke to Eeyore. "That was close. When I flew over you, I thought you were doomed. I called out to warn you, but you couldn't hear me over the noise of the river."

Eeyore looked up at an owl perched on a branch above him. The owl looked calmly back. The little donkey looked down. The water level dropped around him. Muddy boulders poked out of the water. Branches lay up against other big trees. In front of his tree, a massive log lay wedged against it.

He looked back at the owl. "This thing of moving water is called a river?"

"Yes, this is a river. Where have you spent all of your life?"

"I've been in a pasture with other donkeys. They were my friends and—. They all died. They're just bones now. Birds came and ate their flesh. At first, I tried chasing the birds away, but the other donkeys stank. I've been all alone for a long time."

Eeyore bowed his head. It hurt. He was sore from many things. For some reason, talking to the owl had made him hurt more. *Life is short. Soon, I'll quit hurting.*

He looked up at the owl and finished his story. "The storm early this morning knocked down my home and smashed the gate to my pasture. It wasn't much, but it was all I had. I'm looking for a new home."

"I see," the owl said. "Do you have any prospects?"

"Yes, I saw some buildings on up the shore of this big lake."

"There might be a good building for you there. How old are you?"

Eeyore stood up tall. "I'm old enough. I must be almost two."

"Almost two."

"Yes. Of course, I must be getting close to dying."

"Donkeys live for many years, but if you are planning on having a home here that might be a problem."

"Living for many years might be a problem? Why's that?"

"No, no, not living for many years. I meant living here might be a problem. There's something going on here that I don't like. There should be more animals. At night, a big plane sometimes lands in the lake. You should go somewhere else."

Eeyore asked, "What's a plane?"

"It's a very big thing humans made. It lands and comes up to the shore near where you are thinking of having your home. Vehicles drive between it and the big building back there."

"What big building?"

"It is back there in the woods. Stay away from it. You might have heard the strange noises coming from it."

"It doesn't matter. Wherever I live, I'll probably die before long."

The owl cocked its head. "You do have a certain... certain outlook on life. How about if I told you I've seen animals fall over as if dead, and all I heard was pfft?"

Eeyore shrugged. The water had drained back to the river, leaving some pools of water and smaller mud puddles. He started picking his way through the mess the flood had left behind. He saw one of the bubbles float by with one of the green creatures. "What are those floating green creatures?"

The owl snapped, "They're fish." In obvious frustration, the owl said, "I've heard a howling of wolves. There's a wolf pack coming here from back over there. Which way did you come from today?"

"I came from over there. I saw the wolves. I fought one of them. I left him floating in the lake. I expect the rest of them will find me and kill me. I hope they die of indigestion."

The owl flew after him and landed above his head on a branch. "Oh, well. I never— In that case, go on over to those buildings. You might be safe over there for a while. *If you have more trouble, go up this river. It branches. One stream flows down from the left and the other stream comes from the right. There is an old man who lives by the stream to the right. He's strange, but he might help you.* He's strange, but he might help you."

The owl flew away. His voice drifted back. "Whatever you do, don't go to the place where the strange noises are. Also, stay away from that plane, the vehicles, and be careful about being seen during the day. Bye and good luck."

Eeyore heard one more thing. It sounded like the owl talked to himself. "This is a bad idea. The boy is going to get killed."

Eeyore continued plodding along. *Luck? I don't have luck except for bad luck. Eventually, it will finish me off.* He reached the road. Eeyore paused. This road looked different. It didn't have anything on it. "Oh well, my life can't get any worse."

The black night didn't answer. Then, an eerie creaking sound came from two dark trees that leaned against each other. For the first time, Eeyore noticed a cold breeze blowing past him. A bitter cold wrapped around his wet body, but the ominous creaking sent a deeper tremor through him. Eeyore walked onto the road and turned to cross the stream. The stream still looked turbulent. A rustling of branches in the woods interrupted his gazing at the stream.

The moonlight glistened off the bubbles with fish in them. The donkey paused to look at them. *Fish. Those green things are fish.* A branch snapped. Eeyore plodded faster.

The little donkey saw a few buildings off to the left. Eeyore slowed to consider them. *I don't think I'll stop this close to that strange place.* Another eerie creaking prodded him to again move faster. Eeyore continued plodding along. Other noises kept him studying the shadows in the dark woods. Roads branched off, but he could see his destination. Eeyore left the road and walked across a big wide flat area. He felt gravel under his hooves and, then, pavement. The gravel had thistles scattered amongst the weeds. *There's good food for me here. This is a long way from that dangerous place. I might be safe, at least for a day or two. Of course, trouble will find me.*

The donkey walked around the buildings. Eeyore remembered

how his original homes had fallen in the storm. *Something has damaged both of these buildings.* The big building looked sturdier, but Eeyore didn't like the big building. *It's too big.* It was bigger than his old barn.

The little one felt just right. Eeyore used a hoof to push the door open further. He would fit right inside the building.

Eeyore didn't know what the black material was in the building or why part of the roof had a big hole. Everything around the hole was black. Eeyore decided to go eat a thistle before going to sleep.

He walked past his new home on the way to a thistle. His right hip brushed against a corner of the building. From behind Eeyore, he heard a creaking sound. Eeyore turned around just in time to see his new home fall to the ground with a crash. *Well, there goes my new home. I should've expected it.*

Eeyore went to eat the thistle. *I guess my next new home will be the big building. Until it falls down.*

He ate the thistle and found his way into the new home. Just before Eeyore went to sleep, he heard a wavering wolf call.

First, one wolf called, "I'm here, but my packmate is missing. I'm here, but my packmate is missing. When are you coming? When are you coming?"

The answering wolf sounded half asleep. "Sleeping. Missing. Keep looking. Sleeping. Tomorrow, first thing tomorrow."

The sleepy wolf added one more thing. "Look out. Look out for a crazy donkey. He's very dangerous."

Chapter Eight

A Scary Night

Bears are omnivores. They eat primarily plants and fruits, but they also eat insects and other animals.

During late summer and fall, bears will eat almost twenty hours a day. They are working to pack those calories on to prepare for hibernation.

Bears are very good tree climbers, but every tree climber knows mistakes can happen.

Pooh pushed on the couch. It slowly slid across the floor of the living room. By himself, he wasn't big enough to move it, but, working with Izzy, they managed. With a thump, it bumped against the wall.

Izzy got up from where she'd pushed. She brushed some curls of her frizzy hair back from her face. "That's far enough, Pooh. Thanks for your help."

Pooh looked around at the changes in the living room. They had moved the couch from in front of the fireplace. Izzy had her sleeping bag in front of the fireplace. *Why would you want to sleep in that?*

He looked at Izzy. "I'm still hungry. I'm going back outside to look for something to eat."

Izzy shook out her sleeping bag. She laughed and said, "Pooh, you're always hungry. What do you think you can find to eat?"

"Plants, bugs, and fruit. I think I smelled some apples outside. I just need to follow my nose. It will lead me to the apple tree."

Izzy said, "Apples? I would like one. I thought bears ate meat."

Pooh sat down on the floor. "My foster parents fed me milk when I was young. As I got older, they fed me more meat, fruit, and plants. I can get by on mostly fruit and plants. They told me I would need to learn to catch and eat other animals. I don't want to. I would rather have friends, but my stomach tells me I should. What am I going to do, Izzy?"

"I don't know, Pooh. When we get to where we are going, I will try to help you find a solution. I need protein, too. Yesterday, I saw some cattle. They seemed to be happy being owned and cared for by a rancher, but I'm getting bothered by the idea of eating something I can talk with. There are some plants that can provide protein."

Pooh stood back up on his hind paws. "Thanks. I'll go out to look for those apples."

The little bear walked over and pushed the door open. The door complained with a slow-long creak.

Izzy called after him. "Pooh, shut the door behind you, please."

Pooh smelled the outdoor air the opening of the door had drawn in. He stepped through the doorway to the outside.

The little bear lifted his nose into the air. Pooh couldn't smell the apples. He almost forgot to close the door. It creaked when he pushed it shut.

Pooh walked away from the house. He couldn't find the apple smell. The little bear sat down and scratched his head. *Earlier, I could smell the apples, but now I can't. What has changed?*

He looked around. Dark silhouettes of the evergreen trees stood around him. Moonlight illuminated some branches. *It's gotten darker.* Pooh tipped his head back to look up. The tops of the trees swayed with a gentle rustle against the night sky. The stars shined brilliantly in the sky. Pooh thought he saw something move through the sky. He tipped his head back farther. He only heard the calm, undulating sound of the river. *Is it the bat?* Pooh lost his balance and fell backwards onto the ground. Again, he saw something skittering across the starry night sky. Pooh sighed. This is comfortable. His stomach rumbled.

Pooh rolled over and stood up. He remembered the smell of apples came from the direction of the lake. That meant the wind had to be coming from that direction. Pooh looked up hill. *Now, that's where the wind comes from.*

The little bear walked down to the road and started walking toward the lake. The Moon had risen up into the night sky. Its light helped him to see things.

At the base of one pine tree, Pooh spotted the white of some more snowberries. They tempted him, but the lure of the apples drew him onward.

As he walked, Pooh considered the different smells. He recognized many, but one eluded his memory, until he remembered the pika. *There must be lots of pikas up wind from here.*

Pooh also smelled something. It was a faint smell, but it stirred curiosity in him. The little bear pushed his nose against his front leg and sniffed. *This odor smells like me. I think it's a bear.* Pooh didn't remember his mother. He'd never seen any other bears. The smell of the bear also brought to mind a warning of his foster parents. "Pooh, be very careful around other bears. Male bears will sometimes eat bear cubs."

The little bear wanted to try to follow the bear smell, but the warning and his stomach won out. Pooh kept walking downhill. The stronger smell of deer carried on the breeze, too. He remembered how fast some of the deer had moved when Pooh hiked with his foster father. *I wonder if they like apples.* Their smell made him think they seemed to be going in the same direction.

Pooh felt a different breeze. It carried different smells. He lifted his nose to better consider them. A wavering wolf call broke the silence of the night.

First, one wolf called. "I'm here, but my packmate is missing. I'm here, but my packmate is missing. When are you coming? When are you coming?"

The answering wolf sounded half asleep. "Sleeping. Missing. Keep looking. Sleeping. Tomorrow, first thing tomorrow."

The sleepy wolf added one more thing, "Look out. Look out for a crazy donkey. He's very dangerous."

Pooh didn't know what a donkey was, but the idea of an animal that frightened wolves frightened him. Pooh stopped.

Maybe I should go back. He carefully sniffed the air. *What does a donkey look like, and what does it smell like?* A different breeze brought him the smell of apples. Pooh took off after the smell.

The winds shifted again, and he lost the smell, but Pooh kept going. He had a good idea of the right direction to go. He crossed the road and wriggled under a wooden fence. Pooh must've pushed too hard on part of the fence. It fell apart with a clatter. The little bear froze. He waited and listened.

Very faintly, Pooh heard the river. *I must be farther from it.* He could hear the whispering sound of the breeze blowing through the trees.

Again, an eddy in the wind brought the sweet smell of apples to him. He smelled the deer and something else, too. A strange odor made his fur stand up. Pooh jumped up onto his paws.

With the agreement of his stomach, the little bear ran through dry grass and weeds. Pooh saw the source of the sweet smell. A cluster of three trees grew out in an open area away from the taller evergreens. Pooh's stomach rumbled in anticipation. He ran forward. The wonderful sweet fragrance of the apples filled the air.

Pooh also smelled deer. Another smell bothered Pooh. It seemed familiar. He couldn't place it. Pooh considered the strange odor. For some reason, it seemed important. He couldn't remember why, but his fur insisted on remaining standing up. His stomach insisted Pooh ignore the strange odor. Pooh reached the trees and started searching under them for apples. He could smell apples, the deer, and the strange odor. Many small round deer droppings lay on the ground, but his nose found only one small piece of an apple.

The deer must've eaten all of the apples that had fallen to the ground. Pooh looked up into the branches above him. In between the trees, he spotted stars in a big gap.

Pooh didn't think of how he'd gotten the honey from the honey tree. The smell of the apples and his stomach's complaint didn't let him think.

The smell of apples grew stronger. He could see small, round, dark shadows amongst the leaves and tangled branches. Pooh didn't worry about his sore paws. He ran to the nearest tree trunk. He reached as high into the tree that he could. Digging his claws into the tree, Pooh climbed the trunk. At first he moved quickly, until his head bumped into branches. The tangle of branches above him kept his head from getting through them.

Pooh looked for the nearest apples. He couldn't see any close enough to reach. With a grunt of effort and impatience, Pooh pushed his head in-between the branches.

His nose smelled an apple so close. He reached out his tongue and managed to lick it. His stomach rumbled in unhappiness.

The little bear shoved and wriggled past the tangled branches. Branches twisted and snapped. With a crunch, smacking, and happy gurgles from his stomach, Pooh made quick work of the first apple.

Pooh's nose happily led him with squeezing, wriggling, and squirming to other apples. They all disappeared with loud crunches of the apples and smackings of his lips. Pooh didn't worry about any of the branches he broke. He didn't worry about how heavy he was or if the branches could hold his weight. Pooh didn't worry about the swaying of the tree.

He paused and looked around. The small, round, dark shadows amongst the leaves and tangled branches had all disappeared. Pooh looked down. He couldn't see any of the small, round, dark shadows below him.

Pooh looked up. High above him, Pooh spotted more of the wonderful, juicy, small, round dark shadows. These apples hung from a branch reaching high above the top of the tree.

Pooh started climbing to get to them. He climbed straight up the branch into the night sky, but the branch started to lean. The higher he went, the more the branch leaned. Pooh kept going. The branch kept leaning. It swayed with his movements. Pooh didn't remember how he'd gotten the honey from the honey tree. Pooh really didn't think. His stomach demanded he get those apples. The little bear really wanted them, too.

Pooh reached for a side branch just above him. A few apples hung from it, swinging back and forth. The branch he clung to swayed harder.

The branch made a noise. Pooh slipped. Instead of reaching for the higher branch, Pooh clung to the one he'd been climbing. The scary swaying continued, and he froze, hoping the branch would stop swinging.

Pooh wanted to wail, but the memories of the wolves, robot, and, especially, the crazy donkey kept his wail from escaping.

The apples bobbed and swung just out of his reach. His stomach complained. The noise from the tree made Pooh think.

If I keep trying to go higher, this branch might break, and if this branch breaks, I'm probably going to fall back down into the tree, and maybe all the way down to the ground. That might hurt.

Pooh still didn't consider how he'd gotten the honey from the honey tree. His stomach insisted he stop thinking and get those apples.

"Hello."

Pooh almost lost his grip at his surprise. He looked. An owl stood on one of the lower branches. It stared back at him. Pooh answered, "Hello, there."

"What are you doing?"

"I've been eating apples. They're wonderful. You should try some."

"No, thank you. I'll stay with mice, small rabbits, and other things. I don't eat fruit."

"Oh, that's too bad. They are nice, juicy, and very tasty."

"I'm glad you're enjoying them, but I couldn't help but notice how noisy you are."

Pooh looked and listened to the night around him. He couldn't see anyone else and didn't hear anything but the gentle breeze and a distant murmur of the river. He smelled the owl, the deer, and the strange odor. "Am I bothering you?"

"No, you are not bothering me, but I thought you might want to know who else might hear you."

"Who?" Pooh guessed. "The deer?"

"The deer might hear you. In fact, I'm surprised they haven't heard you."

"Would my noise bother the deer?"

"No, it wouldn't bother the deer."

"Then why is my noise a problem?"

"Because the robots might notice it or the deer might tell them."

Robots?

Pooh remembered how the robot had killed the wolf. He remembered where he'd smelled the strange odor before. *The robot.* Pooh shuddered. The branch shook more. *I need to get out of this tree.* At that thought, his nose led his eyes back to the few apples hanging just a little too far to get. *I need to get out of here.*

Fear pushed him to descend. Pooh's stomach pushed him to climb higher and get those apples first.

His stomach won the argument. Pooh pulled himself higher. The branch creaked louder.

Pooh eagerly lifted his head to bite down on the first apple. Juice from the other apples he'd already eaten dripped down his jaw. Pooh crunched down on the apple. The crunch blended with a snap from the tree branch.

The tree branch fell. Pooh fell with the branch. It jerked to a halt with Pooh hanging upside down. The apple he'd bit into snapped free from the tree. Pooh finished eating it and eyed the apples of the group. Those apples and all of the other apples no longer hung high above him. Pooh's stomach gurgled happily. He could get all of those apples.

A tearing, ripping sound finally distracted him from what his stomach wanted. Pooh dropped again and stopped just short of the tangled branches below him.

The owl flew away from below him. "The deer and robots will hear all of this noise. It is not safe to be here. I'd wish you good luck, but you need a miracle."

The upside down bear thought. *I need a miracle? What kind do I need?*

The branch snapped off. Pooh fell. He crashed into the branches below. Pooh felt branches digging into his side. One scraped past an eye.

More branches broke. Others just bent and twisted to let him fall. One stick jabbed Pooh under his ribs. Pooh heard a different type of tearing.

He also heard deer and something else.

A deer's voice said, "There's something over by the apple trees."

An odd voice, different from any other Pooh had heard, spoke. It seemed very menacing to Pooh. "Good, we need more animals."

His fall stopped. Pooh hung upside down. Below him, the ground waited. One waving paw brushed the tree trunk. *I could reach the trunk.*

Pooh heard more tearing. He twisted his head up to look at his beloved red shirt. The branch jabbing him in the ribs had gotten into his shirt through a sleeve. The sleeve ripped. Pooh grabbed the branch with his teeth.

My shirt. How can I save it? Pooh tried to pull the branch back out. His weight fought against him.

The voices and footsteps drew nearer.

"You can take this animal, instead of one of us."

The menacing voice said, "The master said to bring back a deer."

Pooh pulled harder. *I'm too heavy.* The footsteps came closer. Pooh remembered getting the honey from the honey tree. *Floating, floating like the fish.*

The weight Pooh fought against disappeared. He pulled the branch free. *I saved my shirt.* Pooh relaxed. He fell from the tree with a loud thump onto the ground.

The menacing voice continued, "You haven't managed to draw in any more bucks. One of you must come with me."

Pooh scrambled up onto his paws. *They're too close. I can't get away.* Fear threatened to freeze the little cub. Pooh looked around for the miracle the owl mentioned.

Above him, the stars still twinkled in the gap between the branches. Pooh floated up between the gap. He brushed against some of the branches. Pooh tried to make as little noise as possible.

Pooh moved slowly. He slid past the highest branches. Over the top of the apple trees, he saw a group of two does and three fawns. What walked with them froze Pooh's blood.

Moonlight glinted off the metallic surface of something vaguely human looking. Its eyes glowed. In terror, Pooh sped through the night sky. Trees, the big lake, and a big hill flew past. Pooh thought he recognized something below him. It looked familiar, but different.

Lights glowed from the windows of a small house. The terror slipped from him. *Home. I'm home.*

Pooh settled to the ground. *I'm safe. I got away.* Uncomfortable thoughts intruded into his joy and peace. *I promised to protect the others. I promised to catch the thieves and to retrieve the stolen crystal.*

His heart had kept his paws moving toward the door. The porch creaked when he stepped onto it. *I promised Dad and Mom I wouldn't try to come back this year. I better leave or I'll be in trouble again, but I don't want to leave. I miss them.*

The door opened. Light spilled out onto the porch and all around Pooh. He heard the gasps.

"Pooh! It's our Pooh."

His foster parents ran to him. They knelt and hugged him. For a long time, no one said anything, but, then, the questions started. They led him into his home, and Pooh told them everything that had happened.

"Pooh, you're a hero. Are you sure you're okay? You don't have any injuries?"

The little bear pointed at his ragged shirt. "I've ripped my shirt."

They hugged him again. "Shirts can be repaired or replaced. The most important thing is that you are safe. We'll let the authorities know what's going on. We've been wondering about that big plane landing in the lake at night. It will take a week or two, but we'll get some help."

Pooh hung his head. "My friends can't wait a week or two. They're in danger, and I promised to help them."

They talked some more. At first, neither of them wanted Pooh to go back, but, finally, they agreed. "Pooh, you're growing up fast."

His dad held his hand over Pooh's heart. "Pooh, you're growing up in here. That makes me happy. Be careful. Warn your friends. Try to keep them from doing anything foolish. Don't go near the lodge by the lake."

His dad looked at Pooh's foster mom. Pooh looked, too. She had a very determined expression that Pooh knew well. She said, "We will get help. Encourage your friends to wait at least a couple of days.

Now, before you go, you need to eat something."

Pooh recognized the fragrance. *Honey cakes.*

Later, Pooh drifted back through the night sky. He licked his paws one more time. He hoped that he'd missed some crumbs, but he didn't taste any. *Soon, I'll be back at the cabin.*

A noise distracted him. A plane descended out of the night sky and landed on the lake.

Chapter Nine
Escape

Scientifically, there is no such thing as "luck," but people have always tried to affect their luck. Albert Einstein didn't like how things worked at the quantum level. At the quantum level, we can't determine where a particle is, only the possibilities of where it is. In other words, the quantum world is dominated by chance. What if you could control the possibilities, even if it was unconscious? What if you could make your own luck?

That previous question isn't terribly wild. We can and do affect quantum possibilities. It is strange stuff.

Eeyore, in this story, doesn't know anything about quantum physics. The quantum state of superposition is the normal unexamined state of particles. Many different possibilities of a particle are true until an examination of the particle causes a collapse into only one possibility. When we examine the particle, we make that happen. We change reality. Cool. Right?

A very loud noise woke Eeyore. Startled by a smooth, hard floor, his eyes flew open. In the darkness, he could only make out faint shapes. Unfamiliar smells flooded his nose. The unfamiliar smells and the strangely-shaped objects Eeyore saw in the darkness spurred him to motion. Scrambling on the smooth floor with his hooves, Eeyore struggled to his feet. His heart thudded in a rapid, panicked beat.

Eeyore looked around slowly, remembering the evening before.

Something shook the building. A horrible and unfamiliar noise came from outside. Eeyore seemed to feel the noise vibrating in his bones. He looked through the windows and into the night. Something huge, with bright lights, flew low over the lake and landed. Seeing the thing, the donkey remembered hearing similar but quieter noises from the sky. His heart rate slowed. Eeyore watched as the big thing moved on the water. It came closer but moved out of sight to his left.

The loud noise died away, but other, quieter noises took its place. Eeyore stood watching out the window. Someone screamed. "No, No! Ahhh!"

The donkey stepped closer to the window. He heard other voices. Some sounded frightened. Others sounded mad. He waited, not knowing what he waited for. *I might doze.* Eeyore locked his legs just as he did at other times he dozed on his hooves. At times, he did doze, until, again, the loud noise rattled the building. Eeyore backed away from the window but watched out of it as the big thing moved back into his view, lifted off the water, and flew away.

For a long time, Eeyore dozed on his hooves until, calmer, he decided to lie back down. He drifted back to sleep.

Eeyore stirred in his sleep. Again, he saw his mother lying on the ground, dying. She looked at him. Sadness overwhelmed Eeyore. Everyone else had died. His mother was dying. He would die. Eeyore's mother said, "Promise me, you won't die."

In his dream, Eeyore said, "I'll try, Mom. I'll try." She closed her eyes, and her body relaxed. He woke up. The dream still felt so real. *I'm still trying, Mom.*

Mouth open and with wide eyes, he looked around. Memory of the night before calmed Eeyore. *I'm in the big building. Everything's okay. This is just strange stuff.*

A noise outside pulled his attention to the big windows. A scream erupted from his mouth. "Ahhh! Ahhhh!" *What is that?*

Eeyore scrambled on the smooth floor with his hooves. It took him forever to stand. He didn't hear any more noises. Eeyore looked out the window, but he didn't see anything unusual.

Something huge and metallic lurched up to the window. The poor little donkey backed away from the window as fast as he could. His hooves clattered on the hard, smooth floor. Some kind of metal thing stood outside the window. It looked back at him through the window. It stood at least twice as tall as the little donkey.

Eeyore had no idea what it was. Its face had no expression. *What's it going to do?*

With a crash, Eeyore backed into some shelves behind him. Mildewy papers, boxes, and different things cascaded down and onto him. Eeyore stumbled amongst the things on the floor.

Some of the things had fallen onto his head. *I can't see.* Eeyore almost fell to the ground. Shaking his head, he sent things flying. He heard a crash. Eeyore could see.

The thing had smashed a fist through the window. Glass shards flew everywhere. Eeyore ducked behind a counter.

Eeyore heard a horrible rending, snapping, and cracking. He lifted his head to look. The thing had reached a hand though the window and ripped out part of the wall. More sharp shards of glass flew.

The sight of the strength of the thing almost froze Eeyore in fear, but he wouldn't give up. The little donkey turned, and hooves scrambling on the smooth floor, Eeyore charged for the doorway.

The thing ripped out more of the wall. The little donkey's hooves slipped on the floor. Eeyore almost fell.

The thing stepped part way into the building. In the process, it ripped out more of the wall. Part of the ceiling crashed down onto the thing. Eeyore yelled, "Ahhh! Ahhhh!"

The donkey charged out of the building. In front of him lay the ruins of the first building he had sought shelter in. Eeyore turned to the left and instantly started to run. The lake lay right in front of him. Eeyore skidded to a stop.

Out of his left eye, Eeyore saw the thing half in and half out of the building. Its backside faced the donkey. Eeyore had an idea. He remembered kicking the wolf.

The thing struggled half in and half out of the building. Part of the ceiling lay against the top of the thing. Eeyore ran to it and whirled around.

Planting his front hooves, Eeyore lashed out with his hind hooves. He felt them hit the metal thing. A loud bang filled the air.

Eeyore didn't stop to study the result of his actions. He turned and ran back between the two buildings. Behind him, he heard the thing struggling. The loud, hard thuds of his hooves on concrete echoed off the buildings. This led him away from the lake, the buildings, and, more importantly, the thing. *I've got to get away.*

It also led him straight out into the big, open, paved area. He brushed past a thistle.

A tall human woman with a strange hue of green hair stood in the middle of the paved area. She held a gun.

Eeyore turned to the right and ran. Eeyore had seen humans long ago, about a year and a-half, when he was just a foal. He had seen a human shoot a gun at a coyote. The coyote had died.

His hooves made a familiar hard thudding sound on the pavement. Eeyore's laboring heart threatened to pound out of his chest.

In front of him, a few trees grew next to a finger of the lake. The finger came farther than the building. *I'll have to run around the end of it.*

With his left eye, Eeyore watched the woman. With his right eye, he watched for the thing. The woman lifted her gun and aimed it at him. In shock and full of fright from everything, Eeyore lost his footing. The ground briefly turned slippery. He stumbled. *I never stumble. What horrible, terrible, terrible timing. I'm going to die. I'm sorry, Mom. I've tried.* Eeyore started to fall. He heard a sound.

Pfft.

He saw something traveling at him and felt a brush of the thing just passing over his falling back. Scrambling, Eeyore caught himself from falling and ran faster.

The woman yelled something. She sounded angry. *Is she yelling at me? Does she want to talk with me?* The little donkey didn't want to talk. Eeyore ran harder. His breath came fast and hard. Terror had opened his eyes, revealing the red around the white of his eyes.

The expanse of the pavement seemed to go on forever. Slowly, all too slowly, Eeyore crossed the pavement. Ahead of him and past those few trees by the finger of the lake, a hill covered in dark-green, evergreen trees rose up toward a ridge far above him. *I've got to get into those trees.*

Eeyore drew nearer to the small group of trees next to the lake. *That hill looks steep. Is it too steep? How fast can I go up it?*

She's trying to kill me. I'm probably going to die, but I'll die trying. Eeyore felt his heart burning in his chest at a memory. *Son, promise me you will never give up. I promised. I will never give up, Mom.*

Eeyore's left eye watched the woman. She yelled something else. She did something with the gun. His right eye watched for the thing.

The little donkey angled toward a gap in the small group of trees. *That could give me a little shelter.* His right eye gave him bad and good news. The thing walked unevenly from behind the building.

81

Good. I hurt it too bad. It can't get me. His hope evaporated as it started to run.

Behind him, Eeyore saw the woman lift the gun. She's going to shoot. How can she miss again? The little donkey looked at the gap between the trees. *It's close. She missed last time because I stumbled.*

Eeyore jumped for the gap. He heard the noise.

Pfft.

Eeyore fell into the branches. Rolling with the fall, he rolled back onto his feet, jumped up and ran.

His hoof beats changed from hard thuds to crunching sounds. His eyes verified the change. *I've moved from running on pavement to running on gravel.* The donkey could better see the slope climbing toward the ridge. *This is bad, really bad. It gets steep really quickly. I won't be able to run up it. The lake is to my right. I'll need to go to my left.*

Briefly, Eeyore thought about jumping into the lake and trying to swim away. *It would be easier for her to shoot me, and that thing might be able to swim.*

Boulders of various sizes lay scattered about the base of the hill. Smaller trees grew amongst the boulders and even out into the gravel.

Eeyore ran closer to the water. With his left eye, he watched for the woman. He had to be more careful of his footing. With both eyes, Eeyore also kept watching the ground. *It wouldn't do to fall.*

The water lapped peacefully against the shore. In the shallows, his red-rimmed eyes saw small fish peacefully swimming. These fish weren't green. *This would be a wonderful home if I wasn't about to die. The sun felt good on his back, and a gentle breeze carried the smell of pine trees and other things. This is a better place to die than my pasture.*

Eeyore heard the woman yelling. He saw her from behind the trees. The little donkey had run from the behind the trees and back out into the open. *She'll have a clear shot at me.* The woman did something to her gun and lifted it up.

He heard branches snapping behind him. The thing burst through the trees and ran after Eeyore. Two birds flew in from the lake. They flew over the donkey toward the woman.

There's nothing to jump or dodge behind. That thing is too close. I don't have a chance. If she doesn't shoot me, this thing will get me.

He heard the strange noise again.

Pfft.

Something hit the ground under him. It ricocheted away. It was small and had a splotch of something white on it. In that second of a glimpse, it looked like bird poop on the thing.

The woman screamed in frustration. Pooh heard and saw her throw her gun on the ground. *That's three times she's missed me. He heard one of the birds.*

"I tried to poop on her gun, but I missed it."

Inspiration gave Eeyore hope. *I'll probably still die, but I'm trying. I'm trying. I'm trying.* He would try something impossible. Eeyore yelled up at the birds, "Please help me. Try to poop on the face of the thing chasing me."

Eeyore ran as fast as his short legs would go. The thing closed the distance. A bird swooped at it. Something white hit the thing's face. *The bird's poop hit it. The bird's poop hit it.* The thing stumbled and fell.

It rolled into the lake with a splash. *I hope it can't swim.*

Eeyore didn't believe what his right eye had seen. It couldn't be, but it was. *You've been pooped. You've been pooped.* He wanted to sing. *I want to celebrate. You've been pooped. You've been pooped.* He'd never felt this good. Not since... How did the bird manage to do that?

Mom, I'm doing it. I'm surviving. His emotions crashed back down. *I'll probably trip and break my neck. The woman will shoot me. Then, the thing will rip me apart. I'll probably die slowly and in great pain.*

Eeyore didn't let his doubts and fears stop him. He bravely continued his race for survival. The thing splashed in the water. *I damaged it by kicking it. I hope this fall hurt it even more.* The woman had picked up her gun and ran toward Eeyore and the ridge.

I hope she damaged her gun. Eeyore almost stopped running as he realized how much hope he felt. *This is crazy. How haven't they killed me?* The thing no longer splashed in the water. It had gotten to its feet, and it waded out of the water. *It's starting to run again. Oh, no. Is it slower?*

When do I turn? The sooner I turn, the better chance the woman has of shooting me, but if I wait too long... The woman moved into Eeyore's blind spot, directly behind him. He turned his head just a little. *She's messing with her gun while she runs.* Eeyore had a wild thought. *Maybe she'll trip and fall.*

The thing is coming slower, but it is after me again. If I wait too long, I'll be dodging around the boulders. That'll slow me down. The woman will be able to get closer. In a wild burst of hope, Eeyore wished the woman would trip, fall, and trip the thing. It would fall, and Eeyore would escape.

On one level of his mind, Eeyore thought of his possibilities. *They won't trip.* On another level of his mind, the little donkey cried and screamed. *I promised. I can't fail. There has to be a way.*

84

After the amazing success of the bird, Eeyore looked at the boulders ahead of him with new longing.

Those boulders had fallen down from the ridge. There had to be more boulders that might fall. *Is there a boulder that teeters on the edge between falling or staying stable? How crazy would that be if a boulder, just at this moment, fell and hit the thing?* Eeyore had never had such a flight of fancy combined with hope, but the stress of the last day and this situation pushed him over the edge.

I think I've gone crazy. Even if a boulder miraculously took out the thing, I'd still be stuck trying not to get shot. What terrible luck to be caught out here in the open. What an easy place to get shot. I might as well stand still and help her. I have such terrible luck. Still, I can't give up. I promised Mom.

The bird was just amazing, but with my terrible luck, I don't stand a chance.

I'm doomed even with the bird helping me out. As if to certify the thought, the bird flew over him.

"Somehow, I got lucky and nailed it, but we're both out of poop. The thing is back on its feet and starting to gain on you. I wish we could save you. Sorry. Maybe your death will be quick."

The possibility Eeyore needed was just very wild and nearly impossible. Of course, very few things are really impossible. Still, the chances of a boulder breaking free at just the right time and bouncing down at just the right angle to hit the thing had to be vanishingly small.

The stubborn little donkey kept running. *I'm going to die, but I won't make it easy.* He kept an eye on the thing. When it got into range, he would kick it. Of course, then, the woman would shoot him.

Maybe, I could kick the thing and a boulder would take out the woman. I've absolutely, positively gone crazy. If I'm crazy, will it hurt less when I die?

Eeyore turned to the left. He knew it would help the woman run closer for a bit, but he couldn't help it. *I'm running right in front of her. This time she can't miss.* If Eeyore had tried climbing the slope, he would've slowed down, and then she could've take her time killing him. *I had to turn.*

Now, he saw both the threats to his life with the same eye. The thing continued to gain. The woman held the gun at the ready and closed the distance.

She hadn't tripped. *I knew better than to hope for that. I've got terrible luck. I'm doomed.*

One of the birds yelled, "Look out!"

Eeyore screamed, "What can I do? They're going to get me."

The other bird yelled, "Look out! Rocks."

For the first time, the little donkey noticed a rumbling growing louder. His right eye caught the sight of a boulder about the size of his head bounding down at them. There were other smaller rocks. The shock of seeing what he had hoped for almost caused the brave donkey to stumble and fall. It did make him slow down.

Eeyore seemed to feel time slowing down. *Is this what happens before you die?* His left eye told him the thing had gotten so close it could hit him.

His right eye told him the head-sized boulder would hit him. Eeyore saw the thing leap at him. Both of its dangerous arms reached for the little donkey.

Eeyore dodged toward the hill. The boulder flew at him. It just missed him. Eeyore heard the boulder hit the thing with a crash.

The thing hit the little donkey. It hurt, but Eeyore stubbornly refused to fall. Eeyore managed to slip from under the limp thing. More rocks continued to fall. Small ones hit Eeyore. They hurt. He

86

tried to find protection. Through the flying missiles, the little donkey found safety behind a big boulder. His left eye had been watching the woman.

She brought her gun up. The woman walked closer. *She's so close this time. How can she miss? Maybe a rock will hit the thing she's shooting at me. I should move.*

The avalanche of rocks died away. *So much for that hope. She's got me. I'm stuck up against this boulder.* Eeyore spotted one more rock. It must've bounced high off the ridge.

The rock arced high through the sky. Eeyore decided to jump just when he heard the gunfire. *Maybe, I'll get lucky. That's not very likely.*

The woman had come so close. Eeyore could see her mad expression.

The rock fell, and Eeyore realized it fell toward the woman. *Maybe it will hit her.* He hoped with all his heart that it would. Eeyore decided he'd waited too long. He jumped.

The rock missed the woman. The gun fired. The rock hit it.

Pfft.

The gun shattered.

Eeyore ran away.

Chapter Ten

A Surprise Visit

Black bear cubs are not inherently clumsy, but like all animals they are still developing their coordination and skills.

Those cubs are confident and good swimmers. If they have the opportunity, black bear cubs will spend time frolicking in the water. They are also natural climbers, but like all of us when put into new and unusual environments, accidents can happen.

In late summer, bears spend most of the day and night eating.

Pooh waved his four paws trying to run away. A horrible monster called a donkey chased him. A noise shook him from the nightmare. *What's that noise?* Next, Pooh tried to remember where he was. Just yesterday, Pooh had awakened at his foster parents' home. Pooh remembered going to Farmer's home and the honey. He smiled and patted his stomach. Pooh's stomach rumbled. *Oh, my stomach woke me up.* The dream faded, but the memory of the frightening donkey didn't leave his mind. Then, Pooh remembered everything else.

He rolled over and stood up on his hind paws. *I hope I don't meet the crazy donkey.* Pooh had slept in the same room with everyone else. Izzy and Annie still slept. The couch stood over against a wall. At the other side of the room, a table stood. A pot with a dead plant rested on the table. The dead plant hung from the pot and over the edge of the table.

When Pooh looked at the pot, he had a bad feeling. Someone should move that pot. The little bear was clumsy. Pooh had already had one bad experience with another pot in the house. He thought back. It hadn't been all bad. *I did make the others laugh.*

Other than the front door, the room had one exit. It led into a hall, the kitchen, a bathroom, and two bedrooms. In a corner, by that exit, a small bookshelf stood with lots of things on it.

Pooh looked around the room again. He didn't see P'Nut or the weasel. *Where have they gone?*

He remembered seeing the robot. Pooh remembered the wolves howling in the night and what they'd said about a crazy donkey.

Pooh didn't like the idea of a crazy animal that could scare wolves. *I should tell the others about the crazy donkey.* Pooh looked down at Izzy and the dog. *How did they sleep through the noise of my stomach rumbling? How did they sleep for so long?* He had only slept for a few hours. Pooh heard another noise. It wasn't that loud.

The little bear looked toward the door. The noise came from outside. *I better go see what's out there.* Pooh hesitated. *It might be the robot that took the wolf or it might be the crazy donkey.* What would a crazy donkey look like? It must be a horrible, big monster. *Maybe, I could just peak out the door.*

Pooh walked toward the door. He'd just reached out to the door when P'Nut appeared halfway up the door. The squirrel finished his jump into the room.

All tensed up from his fears, Pooh let out a scream, "Ahhh!"

The little bear jumped back from the strangeness and the surprise of a squirrel going through a solid object. One of his paws didn't move fast enough.

P'Nut said, "Look out."

Pooh tried to catch his balance, but, instead, he bumped the potted plant over. It fell over on the table and rolled. Pooh tried to make his paws move faster, but he could feel himself falling. "I heard a noise."

"Yeah, there's a vehicle outside. A woman and the girl who showed us this cabin drove up in it. Pooh, you're going to fall, and that pot is going to fall."

Pooh kept backing up. The pot spilling dirt rolled to the edge of the table and fell. The little bear reached with his left paw and somehow managed to snag it. The pot wanted to roll out of his paw. Pooh tossed it up. He kept backpedaling, trying not to fall over backwards.

The squirrel stood, watching the bear's crazy dance.

Pooh caught the pot with his right paw. He started to use his other paw to keep it from falling, but, instead, Pooh finished falling. He went down. The pot went up. Pooh landed on the floor on his bottom with a thump. The pot came back down. It landed on Pooh's head with a crash. Dirt and pieces of pot poured over him. The dead plant draped over his head. Pooh asked, "What do you want?"

P'Nut pointed behind Pooh.

Pooh tipped his head back to look upside down behind him. The remains of the pot fell onto the floor with smaller crashes. The dead plant shifted on his head. The small bookshelf behind Pooh wobbled but stopped moving. Unfortunately, a big book on the top wobbled toward the little bear. Pooh didn't think of the results of his next effort. He leaned farther back to try and catch the book before it fell. Instead of moving from wobbling to falling, the book surprisingly stopped wobbling. Pooh didn't stop leaning back.

Pooh tried to stop leaning back, but he'd leaned too far. The bear fell back against the bookshelf. It tipped over with a crash, spilling everything on him.

From the mess, Pooh repeated his question, "So, what do you want?"

P'Nut tried to talk. "I... I... Pooh, you're a crazy bear. You're a silly, little bear."

"Yeah, I get that a lot. I'm clumsy. My foster parents told me bear cubs shouldn't be as clumsy as I am. They said I was an overachiever."

"Yeah, a bit, Pooh, but, it's okay. I just came to wake up Izzy. I'm surprised you didn't wake her up with all that noise. The weasel's outside, watching the people."

"What?" There was something about the squirrel that Pooh really didn't like, and it bothered him. *I like everybody, except for maybe the weasel, the wolves, the robot, the deer, and that man in the helicopter. What's happening to me? I used to like everyone I knew.*

P'Nut ran over to Izzy. "Hey, Izzy. Time to wake up. You don't need more beauty sleep. You're already beautiful."

Pooh rolled over. Other things fell onto the floor with more crashes. "I don't think they're waking up very easily."

P'Nut looked back at Pooh and waved a paw at the mess. "If they wouldn't wake up after that, we're going to have to take extreme measures."

Pooh got up onto his paws. He shook off the debris, but the dead plant refused to fall off his head. Pooh walked closer to the sleepers.

Izzy groaned and rolled over.

P'Nut said, "Pooh, grab her sleeping bag down there by the end with your mouth. Be careful, be really careful you don't bite Izzy, and pull on her sleeping bag. I'm too small, or I would do it."

Pooh wanted to argue. He didn't like this squirrel giving him orders. Instead, he just muttered, "Oh, bother." He gently took the end of her sleeping bag in his mouth and bit down. After he knew he didn't have a foot or toe in his mouth, Pooh pulled. He didn't accomplish much. *I wish I was not such a little bear.* The little bear tried again.

P'Nut shook his head. The little squirrel jumped over Izzy and ruffled one of Annie's ears. "Wake up, Annie."

"Huh. What's going on? Is there a problem?"

"Just lick Izzy's face to wake her. I need her help."

Pooh planted his hind paws. He leaned over and again gathered part of the sleeping bag in his mouth. Pooh pulled as hard as he could. This time, when Pooh pulled, he lost his balance.

The little bear let go of the sleeping bag, but it was too late. Pooh fell forward onto the top of his head, flipped, and landed on his back on Izzy's legs. Somehow, the dead plant remained on his head as he did the forward roll.

Izzy sat up with a start. "What's going on? Is there a problem?"

Annie sat beside her and said, "That's just what I said when they woke me up."

P'Nut shook his head at Pooh. "You're a silly bear. Izzy, there are some people here. I need you to come with me. People don't always listen well to a squirrel."

Pooh nodded his head but didn't speak. *Makes sense to me. I don't like listening to you.*

Izzy looked at Pooh. "What are you doing? What's that dead plant doing on your head?"

Pooh tried to think of a non-embarrassing answer. "I think it likes me."

Izzy crawled out of the sleeping bag. "You funny bear, I like you too." She paused and added, "Pooh, I didn't thank you yesterday. Thanks for saving my life and stopping the big boss from getting Annie."

At first, Pooh didn't know what to say. *I'm not a hero.* He'd just done what needed to be done. After an awkward silence, Pooh finally said, "You're welcome. Everyone else did their part." After he'd answered, Pooh remembered what his mother had said. *"Pooh, you're a hero."*

Izzy stood up. "Okay, let's go." She followed P'Nut out the door. This time, P'Nut waited for her to open the door before he went out. The door shut behind them.

Pooh said, "Well, Annie, it's just you and me, now. Everyone else is out there taking care of us."

Izzy opened the door and stuck her head back in. "Annie, could you come with us?"

Annie jumped up and ran out the door. Pooh patted his stomach. "It's just you and me, now. Everyone else is taking care of us." *I don't really think I'm a hero. A hero would be taking charge of things. I'm not a taking charge sort of person.*

His stomach rumbled. "No, I don't think they're getting us some honey. I know. You're hungry. You're always hungry." *If eating was the thing of heroes, my stomach could be a hero. It would be taking charge of all the food.*

Pooh could smell the food in Izzy's backpack. His stomach really wanted more food.

Pooh looked at the closed door. *They might need me, but probably not.* His nose pulled his look over to Izzy's backpack. Pooh looked again at the closed door. *I don't care if they don't think they need me or not. I want to know what's going on. Plus, getting outside would keep me from exploring what food is in Izzy's backpack.*

He jumped to his paws and ran out the door. Outside, the tall trees didn't look nearly as dark and spooky as last night. Sunlight brightened the tops of the tallest trees. A tall, red-headed woman lifted something out of the back of a truck. "When this dear young girl told me about your situation, I said to myself we needed to bring you some supplies."

The girl who'd been so nervous last night and had told them they should leave, stood behind her. The girl didn't have any expression on her face. The girl said, "You should stay. Grace and I brought you enough supplies for a week, and we have more if you need them."

Pooh stopped. *What did she say last night?* He thought for a minute to be sure he had it right. *"It's dangerous. You should leave early tomorrow."*

He scratched his head in thought. *What's going on?*

A robin hopped through the tall, brown grass and the weeds.

Izzy came running up the sidewalk carrying a box full of stuff. "Oh, Pooh. I looked in this box, and you're in for a surprise."

P'Nut stood by the woman and the girl. "Thank you for the food and other supplies. You're right. This is a beautiful area. We'd love to stay for a while. You've been very kind."

The woman said, "You're welcome. I think that suit jacket looks great on you." There was a pause, and she added, "I think there's more to you than meets the eye." The woman and the girl climbed into the vehicle. "This is a busy morning. I need to go check on someone else." Then, they drove off.

The sound of the vehicle slowly died away. The robin flew across the road. P'Nut ran back to the cabin.

Pooh stood watching them go. His stomach rumbled. *I know. You want us to follow the food. Why did they bring us food? And when did I become so cynical?* Pooh knew the answer to the second

94

question. *Coyote.* "Stomach, you're going to have to wait."

"Hey, bear. Do you always talk to your stomach?"

Embarrassed and wondering who had spoken, Pooh looked around. After a second, he remembered the sound of the weasel's voice and looked down.

The weasel looked back at him. "We need to be finding that crystal. Let's go check out this Grace person."

"What about your friend, the wolf?" *Good, let's not talk about my stomach.*

"He isn't a friend, just an acquaintance."

Pooh asked, "Did Grace talk about anything that might help us?"

"That woman told P'Nut she lives down by the lake, and she said there's a dangerous, crazy old man on the other side of the river. Other than that, she didn't tell us much. I say, we go find where Grace lives. Do you want to go with me?"

Pooh looked back at the house. No one else had asked him to help. The bear thought about what the weasel had said. Pooh wanted to scratch his head as he thought, but with his new cynical perspective, Pooh didn't have to think long or hard. He saw something in the weasel's words. *How can I change his mind? I don't know much about this weasel. I'll have to be careful. I'll have to get him thinking.* "Okay, but I think we should try to find a way across the river."

Before Pooh finished talking, the weasel asked, "Can I ride on your shoulder?"

Pooh said, "Okay," and dropped to all fours. The weasel ran up onto his shoulder.

The weasel said, "Why would you want to find a way across the river?"

Pooh thought as he stood slowly up on his hind paws. *Good, he asked a question, but I don't want to answer him. I need to lead his thinking.* "Which way did the woman drive away?"

"She went to the left."

"Did you see which way the robot went with the wolf?" Pooh shuddered at mentioning the robot. Last night, he'd come entirely too close to that robot.

"He went to the left, too. Do you think the robot is working with her? I could look for it when we find where she lives."

Pooh scratched his head. *If only I could think faster.* "I don't trust Grace. She could be using or working with the robot. I used to like and trust everyone I knew, but I'm learning people are all different with different reasons for what they do. Even nice people are not always going to do nice things. With some people, it's really hard to know if they are really nice. The truth is, I don't trust you or anyone in our group."

"Smart bear. I wouldn't trust me. I trust Annie and Izzy, but I have a soft spot for females."

Pooh said, "I trust them a little bit but not to make decisions. They almost died."

The weasel shifted on Pooh's shoulder. "If you don't trust this Grace, why don't we try to follow her? There don't seem to be very many people up here. We could find where she lives, and I could investigate her home."

Pooh walked to the left. *This is the direction the weasel wants to go, but it's also the direction I think the bridge will be. When my dad brought me up here yesterday, there were no other roads past here. This Grace wouldn't have warned us if we couldn't find the way to the old man easily.* Pooh heard the river. He heard a branch snap. The little bear looked, trying to spot the source. *I hope it isn't the crazy donkey.* Slowly, he wandered from the edge of the road and

96

into the trees. Pooh could see some houses. "Did you notice how the girl acted? Yesterday, she told us we should leave and that it's dangerous. Today, she said we shouldn't leave. I think it is dangerous here. I think Grace isn't worried about us, and, for some reason, she wants us to stay. I think she's making a plan to take care of us, and by 'take care,' I don't think she has our best interests in mind. She must have a reason for being so confident. I think we should be very careful about her."

The weasel said, "I get it. You're scared of her. You're over thinking the situation. I'm not scared of anything or anybody, and I know some pretty dangerous people. I'm not worried about Grace. Women tend to like me. I still think we should check her out."

Pooh couldn't be sure, but he thought he saw another road ahead of them. "Did you notice how Grace tried to scare us from talking to the crazy, old man? Grace isn't frightened of having us here, but what she said about the crazy man tells me she's frightened or at least worried about us talking to the crazy man."

"What? What do you mean?"

"First, I don't trust Grace. Second, if she's warning us, trying to scare us from finding and talking to this crazy man, then I think she's frightened of having us talk to this crazy, old man. I want to go see that man."

"That makes a surprising amount of sense. Why didn't you say that, in the first place, instead of just suggesting we look for a way to cross the river? I'd rather first find where Grace lives, but I'll come with you to check out this man."

"Thanks," Pooh said.

Chapter Eleven

Eeyore Gets Lost

There is so much we don't know about interspecies cooperation and friendships. For decades, researchers were trained to not anthropomorphize or attribute human characteristics to animals they studied. That training slowed our understanding of animals and their relationships with each other. It turns out, humans and animals have much more in common than we once thought. How much do we not know, and how weird could it get?

Eeyore ran. He didn't know where he ran to, but he did know what he ran from. Branches whipped past scraping his sides. One hoof hit something. Another hoof stepped into a hole. Eeyore stumbled. He struggled not to fall but didn't succeed. He fell hard and rolled. A big tree trunk stopped his roll. All four of his legs stuck straight up into the air.

A little, fat chipmunk looked down at him from the tree trunk. "Why are you upside down?"

The little creature didn't wait for a reply. It scampered away. Eeyore lay still, breathing hard. The little donkey didn't hear any sounds of pursuit. *How did I get away? I don't have that kind of luck.*

Tall trees surrounded him. Bushes filled the spaces in between them. Small patches of sunlight brightened the shadows. A gentle breeze blew past. Eeyore recognized a level clear path as a road. Small branches and other detritus covered the road.

Slowly, his mind took in his surroundings and shifted out of his terror. Eeyore tried to logically assess the situation. *The metal thing got hit by a boulder. I don't think it is getting back up. The woman's gun got destroyed. She can't shoot at me anymore. Could it really be that my luck has changed?*

A sharp pain hit his hindquarters. His hind hooves lashed out. Eeyore's legs jammed into a bush behind him. *Nope, my luck hasn't changed.*

Eeyore wriggled and rolled. After some scraping of his legs, he carefully climbed up onto his hooves. *I survived a situation that should've killed me. I can do this. Life doesn't have to be horrible or short. I can forget about the skeletons.* Eeyore lifted his head and looked at the beauty of the forest around him. Something caught his eyes. Eeyore looked back. In the grass and weeds next to the road, Eeyore saw a skeleton. The little donkey backed up. He whirled and ran. He crashed through a bush and onto a different road. That one led to a crossroad. Eeyore went straight, until he had to choose which way to go. The little donkey quickly lost track of the twists and turns.

Eyes wide in terror, Eeyore ran around a bend in a road. In front of him, a massive tree lay across the road. Eeyore turned left and charged through some bushes. Birds flew up. *The owl was right. What was I thinking? There isn't anywhere I can be safe.* Eeyore ran from the skeleton, but he couldn't get away from those in his memories. *Where am I going to go?*

The little donkey slowed. One hoof hit something. Another hoof stepped into a hole. Eeyore stumbled. He almost fell. In terror, he lifted his head. The same skeleton lay on the ground in front of him by the road.

Eeyore turned away. Head low, he plodded on. The memories hung heavy. *What am I going to do? I know I'm doomed, but...* The little donkey walked away and stopped. *I've got to keep trying.* Eeyore stood still trying to decide what to try. He heard the river. *I'll follow the river up. Maybe, maybe there's something for me. It'll probably be a bad choice. I'll probably die a horrible death, but I've got to try. Mom, I'm still trying. I'm sorry I got you and the others killed. This is too hard for me. I need help. I wish I knew where the owl is. He seemed nice.*

The little donkey plodded along, head down. When a tree blocked his way, the little donkey went around. When he couldn't find a way forward, Eeyore backed up and tried a different path. He found the river. Sunlight sparkled off it. *The sparkles look nice, but there's probably another flood coming.* Eeyore turned upriver and plodded along.

Eeyore's head swung back and forth. A thistle brushed against his face. *I might as well eat it. I haven't had anything to eat today, and I need to eat to keep trying. Starving would be bad.*

The little donkey chewed on the prickly thistle and looked around. Other thistles grew in the rocky soil of a small clearing. A big tree trunk rested against two other trees. The trunk lay almost horizontal. Eeyore looked at it again.

Curious, the little donkey walked over to it. He had just enough room to walk under it. At one end, the downed tree's root ball formed a wall. Eeyore walked toward it. Under his hooves, dried leaves rustled. The little donkey turned around and looked back. A tree stump blocked part of the view. The morning sun peeked under the log. *It would feel good to rest in the sunshine.* Eeyore looked with his left eye. A thick bush formed a wall on that side. It only had one narrow hole. He looked with his right eye. A tight group of some kind of small evergreen trees formed a dense curtain on that side. The shadow of the tree trunk fell across the lower branches of those trees. Their branches left only one narrow hole in their curtain. The shadow of the trunk went back to where the upper part of the tree rested against two other trees.

With just a few sticks to cover those two holes, this could be a new home for me. Eeyore stuck his head into the trees and bit off the top of a thistle growing in them. Silently, he stood chewing.

100

A thud stopped his chewing. Eeyore froze. *What is that?* The tree trunk above Eeyore shook. The shadow against the ground changed its shape. He could see a shadow moving on top of the trunk's shadow. The trunk shuddered again. The shadow moved. The shadow looked like the same shape as the metal thing before it got broken.

The thing jumped. It flexed its legs on landing. It looked around. Eeyore didn't even breathe. The thing stood still.

Eeyore refused to breathe. It didn't move. The little donkey felt his legs growing weak.

He locked them into place. They held him just like when Eeyore slept. *If I faint from not breathing, my legs will keep me from falling. I must be quiet.*

Darkness crept at the corners of Eeyore's vision. A loud roar came from the other side of the river. The thing took off running toward the noise.

Carefully, slowly, Eeyore breathed out and in. Another roar came from the other side of the river. This time, it sounded equal parts a roar of rage and a roar of pain. *What was that?* For a long time, Eeyore just carefully breathed.

A memory of what the owl said came to him.

"If you have more trouble, go up this river. It branches. One stream flows down from the left and the other stream comes from the right. There is an old man who lives by the stream to the right. He's strange, but he might help you."

Eeyore waited longer. A bright yellow bird flew into the small clearing. It perched on a thistle and started pecking at a seed head. *If that bird isn't worried, it should be safe. Of course, that thing or another thing will probably find me.* The little donkey left the shelter on the uphill side.

Eeyore walked a little way and looked back. *It would've been a nice home.* He looked back uphill and plodded on. Eeyore used the sound of the river on his left side to keep from getting lost. He stopped at a road. The little donkey saw a bush by the edge of the road. Eeyore ran to the bush and crowded into it. With his left eye, the little donkey looked back toward the lake. The road ran straight for just a bit before curving out of sight. Eeyore didn't see any of the things. Eeyore looked with his right eye at the same time in the other direction. Nothing moved on the road. Eeyore thought he heard something. The little donkey shivered. *I can't just stay here. I have to keep trying.*

Eeyore took a deep breath and ran across the road. The river flowed just down from the road. There wasn't any cover. *I can be seen here from the other side of the river or from anywhere on this road.* Eeyore ran back across the road. His hoof thuds on the road sounded very loud. The little donkey ducked back into the bush. A bird landed on the bush.

"I couldn't help but notice, you seem frightened. Is there danger?"

"Yes. I'm scared. A metal thing tried to kill me. There's another after me. I've been running."

The bird said, "I'll scout for you. We have to work together against predators."

The bird flew away. Eeyore waited, shaking and shivering. Time slowly passed. *Why did I ever leave my pasture? It was a very sad place but safe. I never felt this kind of fear in my long life. It would've been better if I'd died sooner. Then, I wouldn't be so scared.*

The bird flew back. "There are a number of them looking back by the lake. It's safe from here upstream."

"Thank you." Eeyore knew he probably wouldn't be safe for long, but, at the bird's words, Eeyore charged out onto the road and ran up it.

The road curved away from the river. Eeyore saw buildings of many sizes and shapes scattered on either side of the road. The sound of the river got quieter. His hoof thuds on the road seemed to grow louder. Eeyore heard his own heart beating. It felt hard to breathe. Finally, he couldn't stand being exposed out on the road any longer.

Eeyore ran into some trees. The donkey found a secluded spot and stopped to catch his breath. *The bird said it was safe up this way. The things are all down by the river.* Repeating the words of the bird helped to calm him. Eeyore plodded through the trees keeping close to the sound of the river. The little donkey plodded around one bush. In the middle of a patch of clover, a rabbit ate. Eeyore looked around. He didn't see anyone else. It might be safe to talk, but probably no good would come of it. "Hello, rabbit."

The rabbit jumped. It looked around until it spotted Eeyore. "Hello. Who are you?"

"I'm Eeyore. I'm new to this area."

"This isn't a good area to be in."

"I've learned that. I'm looking for the old man. I heard from an owl that the old man might help me."

"An owl? I never trust owls. They are so silent. They sneak up on you when you least suspect them."

Eeyore didn't know what to say. He'd seen owls hunting before, so, he knew what the rabbit spoke of. It had never occurred to him how rabbits felt about owls.

Hoping to avoid talking about owls anymore, Eeyore asked, "Do you know where the old man lives?"

"I've heard mention of him."

Eeyore looked around. Everything seemed quiet, too quiet. "Have you seen any metal things today?"

"I have. The robots are scary."

Panic rose in Eeyore. "Where did you see them?"

"Two months ago, when I was young and fresh on my own, I went down by the lake. My mom warned me about going there, but I didn't believe her warnings. There are terrible things going on down there. It's much safer here. I haven't seen the robots for many days."

Relief flooded Eeyore. "I—"

"Until today, that is. I saw one searching for something. It went down the direction you came from. Did you see it?"

Panic, relief stirred together. Eeyore didn't know what to think. Anxiously, he asked again, "Do you know where the old man lives?"

"The old man, hmmm. My mother said he lives upstream and that he is nice, but I doubt it's true."

Eeyore said, "Thank you."

The little donkey plodded on. He hadn't travelled as far as yesterday, and yesterday the wolves had frightened him, but today the strangeness of what had happened and the terror he felt sapped all his will and energy. Eeyore repeated the only thing he knew that would help. *I will keep going. I will keep trying. I'm trying, Mom. I'm trying.*

From the angle of the shadows and the position of the sun, Eeyore knew it was no longer morning. He walked in the sun as much as he could. It felt good, and it helped calm his shivering. *It isn't that cold. Why am I shivering?*

Eeyore continued. Another bird flew past. Eeyore opened his

mouth to ask it a question, but before he could it had flown past.

Ahead of him, Eeyore spotted a bridge. If any of the things are on the other side and see me, they'll be able to run right across.

Eeyore squeezed into another bush and studied the road ahead of him. *I'll have to cross that road to continue.*

A voice from the bush startled him. "What are you hiding from?"

Before Eeyore could register the question, he jumped out of the bush at the voice.

The voice said, "Whoa. Calm down. There isn't anything to be afraid of up here. I should know. I'm a lookout."

Eeyore took a breath and answered the question, "I'm running away from the metal things." Eeyore remembered what the rabbit had called them. "I think they're called 'robots.' They were looking for me. One tried to kill me."

The voice said, "Tried to kill you? Looks like it didn't succeed. You're a survivor." It added, "Good job. Those things are tough."

"I didn't do much. I kicked it and ran."

"Running is always a good idea. Where are you going?"

"I'm trying to find the old man."

"You are? He doesn't like many visitors. He already had a bear and a weasel visit him. They're an interesting bunch. They're staying in a cabin across the river. I think they have plans."

At those words, Eeyore hung his head even more. "The old man was my only hope."

"There's always hope."

Eeyore looked to where the voice came from. A jay looked back at him. "I say, go ahead. There aren't any robots up here, not now anyway. Of course, when you get close to the old man's camp, he's going to stop you."

The little donkey said, "Okay." He plodded on toward the bridge. *He's going to stop me? I don't have a chance if I try to talk to the old man?* Eeyore's path took him back out into the open. He didn't have anything hiding him from across the river. His left eye saw movement across the river. It was small. *What's that?*

All of a sudden, Eeyore had reached the bridge. Voices from above caught his attention. A formation of geese, flying low, came at him. The little donkey heard their voices.

"The old man didn't even give us a chance."

"I just wanted to talk to him."

"Did you see the garden?"

"Don't even mention the garden."

"The old man wouldn't even talk to us."

"I want to get into that garden."

Why am I even trying? Eeyore stopped at the end of the bridge. He remembered the words of the lookout.

"They're an interesting bunch. They're staying in a cabin across the river. I think they have plans."

Do I have an option? Eeyore lifted his head to look around. *What am I doing halfway across the bridge?* Ahead of him, a squirrel hung from the side of a pole.

It asked, "Hello, I'm P'Nut. Who are you?"

Eeyore started plodding toward the squirrel. "My name is Eeyore. I need help, but I probably won't find any."

The squirrel ran around on the pole. "Why do you need help? Why do..."

Eeyore looked at the squirrel. He had only seen one squirrel before. This one looked different. "I've lost my home in a storm. I'm trying to find a new home, but each home I've found either falls down or is in a dangerous location. I shouldn't expect to find any help, but I need to keep trying."

During Eeyore's explanation, the squirrel ran up higher on the pole and back down, and it ran around the pole three times. At Eeyore's conclusion, the squirrel stopped running. "You're right. You should always keep trying. You can come with me. Our cabin is about as safe as anything around here."

"Okay. I might as well. It can't be worse than anywhere I've been, although it probably will be."

Chapter Twelve

Silly Old Bear is on the Case

Grace is a multifaceted word. It can mean a particularly pleasing movement, manner, appearance, or other pleasing or attractive quality.

Grace also means favor granted one that encompasses forgiveness and opportunity to do better.

In religious use, grace can mean forgiveness and salvation, but in all of these grace does not mean the opportunity to do whatever you want to do. Grace is not an opportunity to be evil.

The sound of a river grew louder. A yellow and black butterfly flew past. Pooh enjoyed the fresh smell of pine trees in the morning air. Again, he noticed a distinct lack of smells of other animals. In front of them, a road ran to the left from the road they'd walked on last night.

This road ran toward the river. Pooh came around a building and saw the road crossed over a bridge. It didn't take him long to reach the road and start crossing the bridge.

The weasel said, "Look over on the other side. Yum, yum. I think those are fish caught in a pool of water."

Pooh looked at the debris on both sides of the river and the pools of water above the river on either side. The red fish swam in a shallow pool in between the river and higher ground. Grass, weeds, bushes, even small trees all lay flat and pointing downstream. *It looks slippery.* Pooh remembered what the girl had said yesterday about the flash flood. He also remembered one of the lessons his foster parents taught him. *"Flash floods are very dangerous. They happen after lightning storms and other heavy downpours."* This looked just like what they had talked about. "There must've been a flash flood. My foster parents—"

The weasel interrupted him. "I don't care about how this happened. I care about those fish, but only because I want to eat them. Let's go. You catch them, and I'll help you eat them."

Pooh's stomach rumbled in agreement. "Okay. I like that idea."

Pooh hurried over the bridge. At the idea of eating, Pooh noticed for the first time that morning how empty his stomach felt. He moved faster.

The weasel must've noticed how fast Pooh started moving. He also must've remembered how clumsy the little bear had been. "Hey, Pooh. I think you should slow down."

At the end of the bridge, alders grew at the edge of the road. Past the small trees, big boulders lined the edge of the roadway. Logs and sticks lay jammed up against the boulders. Down from them, a gravelly swale spread between the higher ground of the road and a slightly higher ground near the river. In the swale, big red fish swam in a shallow pool of water.

Pooh stopped in amazement. A bubble formed around one of the fish. It lifted above the pool. In the middle of it, swam the fish. Gravel floated in the bottom of it. With a splash, it all fell back into the pool.

The weasel said, "Hurry, Pooh. Our breakfast is trying to get away."

Pooh's stomach rumbled. In response, the little bear moved faster. The weasel also responded. He responded to how fast the little bear moved. The weasel jumped. He grabbed a branch, swung, and let go.

He flew through the air in front of Pooh. The weasel did a flip and landed on a big branch jutting out from the log jam. He scampered down it and jumped onto one of the big logs.

Pooh pushed through the alders. The bear jumped for one of the rocks. He landed on it, but Pooh hadn't considered how steep the rock surface would be.

His paws slipped. Pooh flew into the air. With one paw, he caught the branch the weasel had landed on. Desperately, he tried to hang on, but bears don't have a thumb. It was very hard to hang onto.

The paw on the big branch stopped his upper body, but his lower body continued its arc, until his paw slipped loose. Pooh sailed through the air. He could see the clear sky above him. He couldn't see where he would land. The little bear let out a wail, "Oh, bother."

Pooh dropped through the air. He landed with a splash. Pooh rolled over. He stood on all four paws and shook. Water flew.

"Hey, stop flinging water. I'm busy. Strange hunting technique, but it worked."

Pooh looked. The weasel held a fish much bigger than himself. It flopped around, but the weasel held on. He bit into its head. The fish flopped more until, with a last flop, it lay still. "I'll eat its head, and you can have the rest."

Pooh looked down into the pool where other red fish darted about in a frantic dance to stay away from him. Another bubble of water, fish, and gravel lifted up and splashed back. *They aren't as good at floating as I am*. Pooh's stomach didn't want to wait on the weasel.

On all four paws, the little bear splashed after the fish. He sent sheets of water flying into the air.

After one particularly big splash, the weasel complained, "Hey, calm down. They can't get away. Just corner one at the edge."

Pooh considered the little predator's advice. One of the fish swam into a narrower part of the pool. The little bear raced over and jumped, falling across the neck of the narrower part of the pool.

Frantically, the fish swam into the shallows, trying to escape. Pooh rolled and, with a paw, scooped the fish out onto the gravel.

The weasel said, "Be quick. Jump on it. Bite it before it flops back into the pool or the river."

Pooh rolled up onto all fours and jumped. He missed. The fish flopped. Pooh jumped and missed again. The fish flopped faster than the little bear could move.

"Aw, come on, Pooh. This is amazingly sad. You're a bear. Get it."

Pooh jumped again. This time, he managed to pin it. The little bear held the fish down. He tried to be gentle. He didn't want to hurt it.

Weasel said, "Now, you're supposed to bite it."

Oh, that's right. Pooh leaned down to bite the fish, but, with one last wriggle, it squirted out of his paws and down into the river.

Pooh' stomach grumbled. He plopped down onto his rump and wailed, "Oh, bother."

The weasel said, "Wow, you need practice. Were you trying to kill it or let it go?

Pooh said, "I've never killed anything, except for insects."

"You need to practice. This pool of water is perfect."

The little bear looked at the fish swimming gently in the pool and at the dead fish. Much of that fish's head had been eaten. Pooh asked, "Are you done with that fish?"

The weasel looked down. "Yeah. I wasn't too hungry. I had part of the rabbit last night and a mouse this morning."

Pooh thought of hunting. *My parents told me I needed to learn to eat other animals. I'd rather have friends, but my stomach needs more than just plants.*

The weasel jumped away from the fish. "The rest is all yours."

Pooh hurried over. His stomach rumbled in anticipation. Tentatively, he placed a paw on it. The fish squirted out from under his paw.

The weasel shouted, "Don't lose a dead fish. Use your claws to hold it."

Pooh looked at his paw and his claws. They looked sharp. He reached for the fish, but, this time, he didn't just put his paw against the fish. Pooh dug his claws in. The fish didn't squirt or slip away. The little bear set to work.

The little bear looked down at the remains of his meal. *That was tasty.*

"Okay, now that you are finally done, let's go."

Pooh stood up to go. A loud roar came from downstream. Pooh's fur stood up on his back.

The weasel said, "I'm glad we aren't headed toward the lake."

The little bear shivered. The roar sounded way too close. "Let's go. I want to put some distance between us and that roar."

Pooh and the weasel climbed much faster back up to the road. Pooh used all four paws to climb. His one front paw still hurt, but he ignored the pain and moved as fast as he could. Before Pooh stood up onto his hind paws, the weasel jumped onto Pooh's shoulder.

From his perch, the weasel said, "Okay, let's finds this crazy man."

Pooh ran down a road. Another roar echoed from behind them. *I think something is in terrible pain. What made that horrible roar?*

The weasel said, "Let's get off the road."

Pooh agreed. He ran from the road and into the pines. They ducked behind some bushier evergreens and around a house. Pooh paused behind the house.

"Keep going. We'll be getting closer to the crazy man and farther from whatever is making those horrible roars. I'm so glad we didn't look for Grace."

They followed the road but stayed in the trees. Pines grew everywhere. A few other evergreen trees grew near some of the empty houses. Pooh saw a few plants that looked good to eat. Most of them looked dry. He leaned over and munched on one.

The weasel said, "How can you eat at a time like this?"

"I'm hungry."

"If you hurry up, we could stop on the way back and try for another fish. You do need the practice."

Pooh looked back. "I don't look forward to going back."

The weasel said, "We'll be careful."

Leaving the plant, Pooh continued on. He didn't smell anyone or see any activity that looked like someone lived in any of the houses. Another road proved to be a bad choice. There weren't any more horrible roars. Pooh felt like giving up. The fish idea sounded better. A different smell changed Pooh's mind.

Pooh lifted his nose into the breeze. He walked along the road, letting his nose lead him. Ahead of them, he saw a sign across the road. It said, "Making Memories." Pooh didn't understand what it meant. "I think this is it."

The weasel said, "I can't read human signs, but those signs I understand.

Pooh looked around. He saw other signs he couldn't read, "Stay Out. That means you, Grace," and "Trespassers will die." Pooh also saw the signs the weasel understood. A skull had a stick through it. A couple of skeletons swayed from tree branches.

The weasel said, "This is my kind of place. Let's go in."

Pooh looked at him in surprise. "I think the signs," Pooh pointed with his paw at the skeletons, "mean that death awaits us if we enter."

The weasel said, "I'm not scared of anything." He ran under the sign.

Pooh looked at the skull with the stick through it. His heart beat faster. "Oh, bother." *It was my idea to come here.* Pooh breathed deeply in an effort to calm his heart. Pooh tried to order his feet to move, but he didn't move. At that moment, Pooh's nose caught a mix of odors. His feet moved and he crossed under the warning signs.

Pooh's stomach rumbled. He recognized the smells. The little bear stopped. *Is there a garden?*

Pooh looked again. Ahead and off to the side, he recognized some plants. It really did seem to be a garden. Pooh remembered his foster mother's garden. The plants he saw growing together looked like the ones she grew. It would have many good things to eat. Pooh's stomach rumbled. He loved his mom's garden, but it had been absolutely off limits to him. He wanted to help with it, but when she'd given him tools to try, he'd never been able to grasp them. One of his fingers almost worked like her thumb, but he had trouble holding onto things.

Pooh pointed with his paw. "That's a garden. Someone does live here.

The weasel said, "Okay, let's find him."

Pooh said, "Wait."

The weasel turned around. "What?"

"There's someone over there." Pooh pointed at a big stump.

The weasel ran to the stump. A bird flew away.

A little girl's voice said, "You're so cute."

The weasel called, "I found her."

Pooh walked over to the stump. Behind the stump, he first saw a child's head covered in long blonde curls. Coming closer, Pooh saw the rest of her. A little girl with no legs lay behind the stump. She lay on a big board. The weasel had cuddled up to her. She petted the little animal.

The weasel asked, "Hello. What are you doing here?"

"I'm running away."

Pooh looked at where her legs should've been. He scratched his head. "I don't see your legs. How are you running away?"

The little girl laughed a beautiful, tinkling sound. It made Pooh think of bells. "Silly old bear, of course I don't run, but I'm leaving, and that is called running away. I'm running away like this."

The board she lay on started sliding on the ground. The weasel lifted his head. Pooh took a step back.

"It's okay. Don't be frightened. I'm just playing with magnetism. I'm making this board into a giant magnet and that tree over there into another magnet. They attract each other, and I run away."

She grinned. The little girl had freckles sprinkled across her nose. When she grinned, dimples showed up on each cheek.

Pooh wished she would laugh again or grin. Her running away made him think of a question. "Is the crazy old man mean to you?"

She laughed again. Pooh wanted to dance. The sound of her laughter made his heart merry.

The little girl said, "No, he's not mean. He's very nice. I'm Grace. Who are you?"

"I'm Pooh. If he isn't mean to you, why do you want to run away?" *This Grace is much nicer than that woman named Grace.*

"He says the world is too dangerous for me. I don't agree. Even if I didn't have my ability with magnetism, I could get around. I have very strong arms. My parents said my name fits me. Even the crazy old man says it." She grinned and added, "He really isn't crazy. He's old, but it's funny to repeat what you said about him. Anyway, they say I'm too trusting. I don't know what's wrong with forgiving and giving others a chance to do better."

The weasel spoke up, "I agree with them. There are bad people in this world. I work with some bad people. They would hurt you. I think you should go back."

Grace looked at Pooh. She looked very surprised. "Why are you a bad person?"

Pooh looked back in surprise. "I..." He didn't know how to respond. He scratched his head. "I don't think I'm bad. Why do you call me a bad person?"

Grace pointed at the weasel. "He just said that he works with some bad people, and I thought you being with him meant you worked with him."

Pooh scratched his head trying to follow her logic. It slowly made sense. "I didn't think I'm a bad person."

The weasel said, "I wouldn't call Pooh bad. He's naïve and silly at times, but I trust him more than I trust most folk. He's also smarter than he looks. I don't truly trust anyone."

Grace looked back and forth between them. "Oh, I'm glad Pooh isn't bad." Then she asked, "Why are you here?"

Pooh said, "We came here to talk to ..." He started to say "the crazy," but he stopped and changed what he said, "The old man. We hope he can help us."

Grace said, "We've had some trouble with people trying to steal food. He's gotten very protective. He won't want to talk to you."

Pooh said, "Maybe you could come with us and help?"

The little girl said, "I don't think I'd make any difference. Just be yourselves and don't give up." She pointed at Pooh. "I think you should do all the talking."

The weasel said, "I agree. I don't tend to get good reactions from men."

Pooh said, "Okay. thanks for talking with us, and good luck with running away."

The little bear looked away from Grace and up toward the garden. His stomach rumbled, but Pooh paused. He thought of the others. What would they be doing? He hated the thought, but... *Maybe I should've talked to that secret agent guy. I wonder what P'Nut is doing, now.*

117

Chapter Thirteen

P'Nut's Mission

Even without thumbs, eastern gray squirrels have very dexterous front paws. Their paws can also rotate one-hundred-and-eighty degrees. That is why they can run headfirst down a pole or a tree. Squirrels, including eastern gray squirrels, have long whiskers. Those whiskers, called vibrissae, are very sensitive to touch and vibrations. They don't have those vibrissae just on their heads but also in various places on their bodies. As they move, they are feeling everything much more acutely than we can imagine. For P'Nut and other squirrels, that really helps in the dark.

P'Nut looked after the departing truck. He didn't like Grace's choice of words. *"There is more to you than meets the eye."* A memory popped into his mind. *Mr. Bond had said that he had found out about P'Nut because of all the videos online. Whatever did that mean?* He stopped and looked back at the departing lady and girl. P'Nut noticed that the bear, Pooh, stood watching the truck leave.

The little squirrel didn't like having the bear, Annie, and Izzy to look after. *They think I'm some great, special secret agent, but I'm really not. Bond gave me some fancy gadgets, but I'm still just a small squirrel. I'd better stop just watching the bad people drive away.*

Plans, I should make plans for us. They depend on me to get the crystal back. Why did I agree with Mr. Bond? I'm no secret agent. I'm just a little squirrel. P'Nut looked around. *Where is everyone?*

118

What's everyone else doing?

P'Nut turned back and leapt at the door. *One of these times my dramatic entry is going to cause me trouble.* He vibrated through the door and into the cabin.

Izzy held a spoon and a jar with golden liquid in it. P'Nut recognized the fragrance immediately. He stood on his hind paws. With one paw, P'Nut carefully brushed his suit. "I wouldn't mind a small taste of that honey."

Izzy smiled at him and shook the spoon at him. "This is a special treat for Pooh."

Annie said, "I doubt if P'Nut could eat much more than just a few drops. Pooh will never notice sharing that amount. I think you should give P'Nut some."

Izzy grinned. "How much do you like honey, P'Nut?"

"Not as much as Pooh, but it is a great snack."

She said, "Okay." Izzy carefully dipped the spoon into the jar and pulled it back out. After setting the jar down on the table, Izzy walked over, leaned down, and held the spoon out for P'Nut.

The little squirrel carefully licked the honey off the spoon. He loved the sweetness and the flavor wasn't bad either. "Thanks." P'Nut looked around. "Where are Pooh and the weasel?"

Annie said, "They left the driveway right after you came in."

P'Nut screamed, "What? Why didn't you say something? Does anyone know where they are going?" The squirrel didn't wait for a reply. He turned and jumped back through the door.

Outside, P'Nut ran around looking and smelling. *They're gone.* The little squirrel raced back inside. "Okay, they're gone. You two stay here. I'm going down the direction Grace went. That's the most dangerous direction for Pooh and the weasel to have gone. If I don't

119

find them, I'll try to find where Grace lives and make sure Pooh and the weasel didn't get captured."

Izzy said, "What? I thought Grace was very nice."

P'Nut said, "Did you see the difference between the girl last night and this morning? She's obviously terrified of Grace."

Annie said, "I smelled fear coming from her."

Izzy said, "Okay, but wait. We are supposed to be a team, working together. Pooh and the weasel shouldn't have left without talking about it, but you shouldn't either."

P'Nut shifted from side to side. *You don't get it. I'm supposed to be the secret agent. I should be taking care of you.* "Okay, Annie and Izzy, I'm quite concerned about those two, but sure let's take some time. I want to go check on them, and if necessary, try to rescue them. Can I go?"

Annie looked back and forth between Izzy and P'Nut. Izzy stared at the little squirrel. "I think we should go with you."

P'Nut shifted faster back and forth. "How would your coming help? I'm much smaller and harder to see than either of you. I'll blend in with the other wildlife. You two are huge and can't blend in with wildlife. You coming with me is a terrible idea."

Annie said, "I'm sorry, Izzy, but P'Nut does have a point. Also, he could sneak into a building if necessary. You and I can't do that."

Izzy said, "Okay, only you go, but don't get caught, and don't take chances. If you need help, come back for us. Annie could rip the roof off a building. That could be a help. And I... I could—"

P'Nut said, "I'll get going. Yes, Annie could be a big help. If I need that kind of help, I'll be back. While I'm gone don't go down to the lake." He turned to go.

Annie said, "Good luck."

120

The little squirrel jumped and vibrated through the door. Outside the sun shined bright. P'Nut blinked at the brightness. He scampered down the driveway. *That honey helped. I won't need a snack for a bit.* P'Nut jumped onto one of the pine trees, ran up it, stopped, and looked around. More trees, mostly pine trees, surrounded the road on both sides. Toward the lake, P'Nut saw fewer trees. He also saw poles with wires running from them. *I can use them. I'll be off the ground and can run fast. If Pooh went that way, he will probably follow the road.*

P'Nut heard the rushing, splashing sounds of the river. A few birds flew around. He spied a very small squirrel-shaped animal with stripes. He saw a pole on his side of the road with a wire going over the road. Turning his wrists, P'Nut ran headfirst down the tree and jumped to the ground.

Moving swiftly, P'Nut jumped and ran along the road. Even looking for Pooh, the hyperactive squirrel took in everything around him. P'Nut ran over and climbed another tree to check out some houses. P'Nut couldn't see any people. He looked in the windows.

They all looked dark. P'Nut saw a broken window. Between the houses, P'Nut saw a bridge.

A splash echoed from the other side of the river. For a second, the squirrel considered checking it out.

What made that splash? The scolding of a creature pulled his attention back across the road. *That sounds like me.* Looking down, between some branches, P'Nut spotted the speaker another very small squirrel-shaped animal with stripes.

"Look out, there's a hawk. Look out, there's a hawk."

A hawk flew out of the trees across the road. It turned and soared up the road. P'Nut held still, watching it. He hadn't any experience in the outdoors, but he recognized the hawk as dangerous. *If I had been out in the open, especially in the middle of the road, that would've*

121

been very dangerous.

P'Nut waited until the hawk disappeared into the trees far up the road. He ran down and jumped. He stopped and looked up and down the road. Everything seemed quiet. P'Nut turned his ears toward the river. He'd heard something different from over there. *Probably, whatever made the splash is doing something.* The squirrel scampered over to the pole and ran up it. *How do all these poles grow along the road? They don't have any branches or leaves. How do they get wires running between them?* At the top of the pole, P'Nut looked back at the river. He could see the opposite side of the river except where a tree blocked his view.

If that's the silly bear, it should be safe. That's a safe direction. I could check to see if it is the bear, but I want to go check out where Grace lives. The road looked clear. P'Nut didn't see the hawk. He jumped onto the wire. With his tail waving back and forth, he ran on the wire and across the road. P'Nut jumped up onto the new pole. He looked up the road and down the road. The squirrel didn't see any activity.

P'Nut repeated the same technique of running on a wire to the next pole, jumping on to the pole, and watching for danger or anything or anyone moving. Pole after pole came and went.

P'Nut only saw a few birds. He stopped on the top of another post and brushed a needle off his jacket. *I'm the secret agent. Stealthily, I'm approaching the headquarters of the evil villain. I will find the crystal and retrieve it from under the nose of my enemy.* P'Nut resumed running along the wires. He heard the voices of other squirrels scolding a couple more times. They came from the woods, back to his right and toward a mountain.

The number of buildings increased, and the number of trees decreased. P'Nut stopped on a wire. His tail swished back and forth. He looked around, trying to see what bothered him. *There's nothing moving. There aren't even any birds.* Moving slower, P'Nut continued. The road made a slight turn to the left and straightened.

He'd just reached the top of a pole where he could see a lake in the distance when another, bigger, squirrel ran on a wire toward him. P'Nut remembered his only other encounter with a squirrel. It had chased him from its tree. That squirrel had been about the same size as P'Nut, but this one was definitely bigger. It looked different, too. It had more gray and didn't have the cinnamon brown color on the side of its face that P'Nut had.

He said, "Hello, hello."

The other squirrel said, "Hello, hello. Where are you going?"

"Not in your trees. Not in your trees." *There I am repeating myself again, but it does seem to be how other squirrels talk. Would they think I'm strange if I didn't do it?*

"Good. Good. My trees are back there behind me. They go back on the lower part of the hill. I saw you coming. I saw you coming. You aren't from around here. You're different. It's a bad idea to go to that big building down by the lake."

"Where is it?"

"At the next bend in this road and on the left. It's very dangerous. The metal things and the lady keep taking animals. You don't want to go any farther in that direction. All the big animals are gone. They've recently started taking some squirrels. There is—"

A very loud roar interrupted the squirrel. At the terrible noise, both of the squirrels whipped around and looked toward the lake. Everything seemed quiet and peaceful.

A rabbit hopped across the road. It stopped and sat up. A gust of wind blew through a maple tree next to the road. A burst of brightly colored leaves swirled across the street. The rabbit turned toward the lake. In seconds, it sped across the street and into some bushes.

P'Nut turned to the other squirrel. "What was that?"

The other squirrel said, "I don't know what that is coming around the corner, but I'm not staying here." The squirrel moved faster than P'Nut had ever seen a squirrel move.

P'Nut looked back. Something very big ran around the corner of the road. It took P'Nut a moment to recognize it. The thing had something metal on its head and on its back.

In a shocked voice, P'Nut said to himself, "That's a gorilla, but what have they done to it?"

The big animal ran over to a power pole on the other side of the road.

It grabbed the pole and broke it off at the ground. P'Nut gazed in shock. *It's a monster.* The wires running from that pole to a pole on P'Nut's side of the road whipped through the air. Some wires ripped loose. The pole on P'Nut's side of the road leaned toward the other side. The pole the squirrel stood on vibrated. P'Nut looked for somewhere to retreat to.

Shiny, metallic robots marched around the corner. They held some kind of guns. The gorilla flung the pole at them. The wires snapped free. Some of the robots managed to dodge, but the spinning power pole smashed other robots. The red-haired lady, Grace, came around the corner. P'Nut didn't recognize what she held. She did something with it. The Gorilla roared.

This time, P'Nut recognized pain in the roar. The gorilla reached up to the metal thing on its head and wrenched it free. The mighty animal fell over into some bushes and out of view.

The little squirrel shivered. *I'm glad I can't see that gorilla. I can't believe it just ripped that thing out of its head. This is terrible.* Another thought, a very important thought, squeezed past the terror. It echoed in his mind.

P'Nut whirled and ran down the back side of the pole. *I don't want them to see me. I don't want them to see me.* The words of the

124

other squirrel came back to haunt P'Nut. *"They've recently started taking some squirrels."*

In P'Nut's mind, he saw himself wearing a smaller form of the gorilla's metal thing. A shudder ran down his back.

The little squirrel didn't jump to the ground. He kept the pole between him and the horrible sight he'd seen. On reaching the ground, P'Nut ran toward the hill.

He didn't jump like he normally did while running across the ground. P'Nut stayed as low to the ground as he could. He veered his path to take advantage of any bush or slight rise of the ground. *I don't want them to see me. I don't want them to see me.* What had been done to the gorilla was terrible. Another thought pounded in his mind. *That's what they are doing to animals. The gorilla tried to get away. If they catch me, they'll make me into some kind of mutant, half-person, half-machine monster.*

P'Nut ran and ran. His terror kept him going past trees and up the hill. His terror kept him from thinking logically. His terror kept him from hearing a voice. He ran and ran.

"P'Nut, are you okay? This is Bond. P'Nut, please respond."

The little squirrel continued his headlong rush up the hill. He didn't register the words. Again, P'Nut saw the terrible images in his mind. He ran.

The voice coming from the communication device pinned to P'Nut's suit repeated the message again. "P'Nut, are you okay? This is Bond. P'Nut, please respond."

A squirrel, the other squirrel, jumped in front of P'Nut. P'Nut swerved and jumped onto a tree.

The other squirrel said, "I think this is far enough away. No one is chasing you. No one is chasing you." Then, in a curious tone, he asked, "Why are your fancy clothes talking to you?"

P'Nut clung to the side of the tree. He shook from fear. The voice of the other squirrel got through to him. "Huh, huh?"

"P'Nut, are you okay? This is Bond. P'Nut, please respond."

"There it is again. There it is again. You're really strange. You wear clothing, and it talks to you. Are you going to respond to your clothes?"

P'Nut looked down at his suit jacket. Bits of grass and twigs stuck to it. He brushed at his suit, trying carefully to clean it.

The other squirrel asked, "Are you okay? Are you okay? That was pretty crazy down there, wasn't it?"

P'Nut looked up at the questions. His mind kept replaying the scene he'd just witnessed. Still, the questions finally started to get through. "No, no, no. I'm not okay. Did you see that gorilla and what happened?"

"Gorilla? Gorilla? That's what it was? Yeah, it was pretty bad. I'm going to move my food stores to higher locations. No way am I living anywhere close to that crazy stuff below us." The squirrel ran away.

P'Nut responded to the other squirrel, "Yeah, yeah. I don't want to stay around here—"

"P'Nut, are you okay? What is going on? This is Bond. P'Nut, please respond."

P'Nut stopped talking at the interruption. The terror ebbed just a little bit. P'Nut remembered Bond. He remembered the others he worked with. He remembered the promise he'd made to retrieve the crystal. P'Nut remembered Bond selecting him for a very important mission.

P'Nut wanted to run away. He looked down at the communication device pinned to his suit. *I could take it off.* It would be so easy to remove the device and throw it away. P'Nut answered.

126

"Hello, Bond. I'm okay at the moment. I just saw a gorilla wearing some kind of crazy metal stuff. Robots chased it. The gorilla ripped the metal stuff out of its head and died. It was horrible. I'm afraid. I'm terrified. I don't think I can do this. The people who chased the gorilla have the crystal. I don't think I can get it. I'm sorry. I'm sorry. I'm not a very good agent."

P'Nut felt terrible. Before, he'd just been terrified out of his mind. Now, he still felt terrified, but he also felt worthless. *I'm failing everyone. Who am I kidding? I'm no secret agent. I'm a terrified little squirrel.*

Bond said, "You are right."

What? He thinks I'm not a very good agent? "Hey, that isn't fair. I got the crystal from the plane. I rescued the dog, Annie. I..."

P'Nut faltered. His voice died away. *I may be terrified and frightened out of my mind, but I'm not giving up.* "I—"

Bond interrupted him, "P'Nut, my good man or my good squirrel, I am afraid you misinterpreted my words. I meant what you saw was horrible. I agreed with you. What you told me about the gorilla was very bad news. I have good news to tell you. You have succeeded in stopping the NGO for the time being. You have done a great job. Do you feel better?"

P'Nut managed to say, "Yes."

"Good. After finally getting you to respond, the odds of success are better even with your news about the gorilla and the whereabouts of the crystal. You, P'Nut, are very important. In fact, I have recalculated what is important, and while the crystal is still important, you and other creatures like you are more important."

P'Nut opened his mouth, but he couldn't say anything. *I'm important?*

Bond continued. "I have reexamined the data I have access to. A plane has been sneaking into your location. It is part of a Chinese Triad called New Dragons. They are creating an army of animals that can manipulate the laws of physics. They are using that metal thing you mentioned to control the brains of those animals."

P'Nut didn't understand. "Okay. What do you want me to do?"

Chapter Fourteen

The Not So Crazy Man

Physics is fun stuff. It is a lot of fun to wrap your brain around the laws of physics. It's all about finding something well-written to help you understand. In this book, some animals and people have learned how to play with different laws of physics. Imagine if you could do that.

Friction is simply the resistance that one surface or object encounters when moving over another. In physics, it is described as a force that opposes motion between surfaces in contact. What happens if you get rid of friction?

Pooh watched, the little girl, Grace scoot away on her board. *She's awesome.* A thought came to Pooh. *I should've warned her about the crazy donkey.*

The weasel jumped up and ran across the ground.

Pooh followed. He remembered his training. Pooh stopped. "Hello, crazy, old man, we are visitors and would like to talk to you." *Maybe I shouldn't have called him crazy.*

The little bear took a step. His paws slipped out from under him. Pooh landed on his back. The force of the landing knocked the air out of him. When Pooh fell, he started sliding.

The weasel yelled, "Hey, what's happening?"

Pooh looked and saw the weasel sliding, too. The little bear rolled over onto his stomach and dug his claws into the ground. That didn't help. His claws just slid through the soil and plants.

The weasel yelled, "We're headed down to the river."

Pooh didn't understand what had happened. Everything felt slippery. He looked at the weasel. He slid along the same course. Pooh held his paw out. "Can you get onto my paw?"

"No. I can't get any grip on the ground."

The little bear wriggled and stretched. Pooh started to spin on the ground as he slid downhill. He felt the weasel grab his paw.

"I've got you."

"Climb on, and hold on. I've got an idea."

The weasel ran up to his shoulder. "Okay."

Pooh remembered how it felt to float. *I can do this*. At first, nothing happened. He stopped sliding. Pooh floated up into the air. At first, he still spun. Carefully, he turned around and started back. From his new height, Pooh saw a cabin and, standing by it leaning on a cane, an old man. He had white hair and a beard. The old man watched them.

Pooh said, "Please, we just want to talk to you."

The old man turned, and Pooh saw a little boy sitting in a chair. The old man said, "Buddy, push them away."

Pooh felt a force pushing against them. They started moving back toward the river. The little bear thought. He scratched his head. *This force pushing us is the same force the fish use to move after they float. That's how I move.* Pooh pushed them up and to the side.

Momentarily, they could evade the pushing force, but it would find them again. "We just want to talk to the crazy man. Please stop fighting with us."

The aerial fight continued. Pooh felt a headache coming on. He dodged. No answering push stopped them from moving forward. Slowly and cautiously, Pooh drifted them down.

Pooh asked, "Is it okay to land? I'm getting a headache, but I'd really just like to talk to the crazy, old man."

He heard the man laugh and say, "Crazy, am I? Okay. I like your spirit, little bear. Come on down, and we'll chat."

Pooh slowly drifted down. Suddenly, he lost control and fell the last five feet. The little bear tumbled. He landed on his back looking at an upside-down old man. The old man laughed.

The weasel hopped into Pooh's field of vision. "Pooh isn't very coordinated. I've seen him fall on his back a number of times."

The old man stroked his white beard. "He's just a youngster. He's still growing. He'll get more coordinated as he grows up. What do you want to know?"

Pooh had wanted to ask about robots and Grace, but now, other questions populated his curious mind. "What caused everything to be so slick?"

The old man smiled. His face around his eyes filled with wrinkles. Pooh thought it was a friendly face.

"When things move, they have to use or fight friction."

The little bear didn't understand, but he nodded his head.

"Little bear, you might be more comfortable if you roll over and sit or stand."

Pooh rolled over and stood up on his hind paws.

"Why do you stand on your hind paws?"

"I have an injured front paw. It happened long ago. I can stand on all four paws, but it hurts."

The old man nodded his head. "Where did you learn to nod your head?"

"My mother bear died when I was a baby. My foster parents, two humans, raised me. I picked it up from them."

"How do you float?"

"I don't know how I do it. I watched fish do it, and I copied them. They also use something to move themselves. I copied that, but I didn't know what I was doing until that aerial battle. It's some kind of force that I can use to push on things."

The old man nodded. "You can use it to pull on things, too, and yes, it is a type of force, kinetic force. We just call it force."

The weasel interrupted the conversation, "I thought we came here to ask the crazy, old man questions, not to answer his."

The old man laughed.

A small flock of geese circled overhead. The old man pointed at them. "They better not try to land here."

"Why?"

"Geese will destroy and eat the food in our garden. We have had to fight against them a number of times. They don't seem to learn. Maybe we need to have some roast goose."

Pooh asked, "Roast goose?"

"We do have to eat to live."

Pooh asked, "What do you know about Grace and robots?"

The old man frowned. "She's worse than the geese. She is very

132

dangerous. Why do you want to know?"

The little bear looked at the weasel. Pooh waved his paw at the weasel. "We had something important. If Grace has robots, I think she has it."

The little boy sitting in the chair, Buddy, said, "We could help them get it back from Grace."

The old man said, "No, we are safe here."

Pooh asked, "What is this place?"

"We used to be a place for families of children with disabilities to come. We would help them make memories that would be a source of encouragement for them."

Pooh said, "You said it 'used to be.' What happened?"

"When everything changed, and we could understand animals. Three things happened to us here. People in the area got scared of the wild animals, so they left. Also, Grace came. She took over the old lodge. Grace started scaring away folks. She tried to scare me away.

At the same time, some of the children with disabilities learned they could do amazing things by playing with the laws of physics. People became scared of their own children. It was terrible. My children, these that are here with me, were brought here by their parents. This is a refuge for them. That's why I can't help you against Grace. I'm sorry, but my children come first."

Pooh looked around. Other children had come up to listen. Many of them had something that he recognized as a disability. Two sat in chairs with wheels. Pooh remembered the little girl, Grace. "Oh, I forgot something I need to tell you."

Pooh pointed back at the sign. "There's a little girl named Grace out there. She's running away."

The old man said, "I know."

"You know?"

"Yes. She goes the same way each time. We have a friend, a camp robber, watching over her."

The weasel asked, "Camp robber?"

"It's a type of bird, a jay."

"Oh."

Pooh knew what a camp robber was, but from the weasel's voice, he didn't think the weasel understood. "How can a bird protect her?"

"The few animals in the area know us and are our friends. They wouldn't hurt her. If our sentries see the woman, Grace, or any of her minions, they will let us know. We can protect our little girl."

Pooh said, "Good. Grace, I mean your little girl, is very sweet. I'd hate to see her get hurt."

"Thank you."

The little bear scratched his head. "It's kind of confusing having two Graces."

The old man said, "Yes, it can be, but it is a good reminder."

Pooh asked, "What do you mean?"

"People have gotten the word 'grace' confused. For many there are now two uses of the word 'grace.' To some people, 'grace' is a right and is forgiveness and a free opportunity to be as they are. All too often, that means some people are allowed to keep hurting others."

Pooh scratched his head at the partial explanation. "And the other use of grace?"

"It is an unmerited favor and opportunity for forgiveness with the possibility of receiving salvation from the results of doing wrong. It is also miraculous help to do better, but not everyone is willing for the help, and they just revert to making grace the first type I talked about."

The weasel said, "Yeah, and who can give that amazing type of grace?"

The old man said, "I believe that there is only one that can honestly offer and provide that kind of grace. That is God."

The weasel opened his mouth to say something. He shut it. Finally, he just said, "Oh."

Pooh said, "My foster parents talked about God and his help. I try to be willing for it. I want to help others and to have lots of friends." After a second, he added, "'Grace' is a good name for the little girl."

The old man nodded his head, and then he said, "'Grace' is also a good name for the woman. She has been shown grace and has been offered help, but she is determined that she's fine the way she is. That attitude is similar to what other people feel."

The weasel said, "Okay, back to important things that can make a difference. You won't help us. Do you know anyone else who can help us, or do we just go find that woman we're talking about and take back what she took."

Pooh said, "That was important."

The old man held up a hand. "For some, real grace is important, and others don't care. Weasel, I wouldn't advise you to try to take back what she took, but I do know someone who might be able to help you."

The weasel asked, "Who?"

"Another bear. This is a safe time to look for him. He has plenty of food from the spawning salmon. You can find him along the two forks of the Wallowa River. He stays above the main river because he avoids running into the woman or her minions. I used to think he made luck by playing with the physics of possibilities, but he's just very careful."

Pooh asked, "How can he help us?"

"He knows everyone in the area, and he's itching for a fight with the woman. He doesn't like her."

"Great. Thanks."

The weasel said, "Let's go."

Pooh said, "I like it here. I wish I could stay with you, but I need to help these people recover what was stolen."

The weasel resumed his place on Pooh's shoulder. "We should go right back and tell the others what we learned."

The little boy, Buddy, said, "Be very careful about Grace. She's very dangerous. Also, there's a lot of activity down there at night. A big plane comes, leaving things and taking things."

Pooh said, "Thanks." He set off. Pooh kept a careful watch for the little girl, Grace, but he didn't see her. At the bridge, he paused and looked both upstream and downstream. They didn't see the other bear. They didn't see the jay watching for Grace, but Pooh did see the fish. His stomach grumbled.

The weasel said, "Your stomach is loud."

Pooh agreed. He also hated not stopping for another fish. Pooh took one more look at the river. What he saw stopped him. A little bird flew into the water. He watched as it popped up a in a different place. *I could ask that bird if it has seen the other bear.* Pooh wanted to go back, but he knew the weasel was right about the need to return to their friends.

How long had they been gone? What had the others been doing? The more he thought about it, the faster Pooh moved. His paws had been feeling better, but now his paws started to get sore again.

Pooh looked at the trees and down the road, trying to take his mind off his sore paws. A jay flew past. *Is that the camp robber friend of the old man?*

A call tore his attention away from considering the bird.

Chapter Fifteen

Honey

Dogs have been bred to do and be many different things. Each breed is different, and some of them are very different from each other. Training makes a big difference for any dog, but just like a miniature horse cannot be trained to be a racehorse, a Chihuahua cannot be trained to be a sled dog. Every breed has its built-in advantages and limitations. People are that way, too.

"Pooh! Where have you been? We've been worried. We looked all around the cabin. Why did you leave?"

The weasel said to Pooh, "That's the trouble of working with others. They get upset when you don't let them know what you're doing."

Pooh looked at Izzy. She ran toward them. Her black frizzy hair stuck out around her face. Behind her came Annie. The big dog's tongue hung out of her mouth and drool dripped from it.

Annie said, "You found Pooh. Is the weasel with him?"

Pooh answered, "Yes, the weasel is with me. Can we go back to the cabin and eat something? I can tell you what we learned."

The weasel asked, "Izzy, can I ride on your shoulder?"

"Sure." She reached her hand out at the level of Pooh's shoulder, and he jumped onto it.

Annie asked, "What did you learn?"

Izzy said, "You shouldn't go off on your own. We're supposed to be a team."

Pooh suddenly realized one was missing. "Where's P'Nut?"

Izzy said, "After you left without talking to us, P'Nut was terribly worried. He went down toward the lake looking for you and to find where the girl and Grace live." She glared at Pooh. "We talked about it as a team and decided he should try." She accented the rest of her words. "He is experienced at this sort of thing."

Pooh asked, "Grace? Which Grace?"

Annie said, "There's more than one Grace?"

From Izzy's shoulder, the weasel said, "You're getting Pooh mixed up. He really is a nice and smart bear, but he seems to get confused about as easily as he falls down. Let's go back to the cabin and let him eat. Once he eats, he'll probably think better."

Eating sounded good to Pooh. He continued toward the cabin door. "I'm sorry. We met another Grace. She's a little sweet girl with no legs."

Izzy gasped. "No legs! How sad."

The weasel said, "Actually, she's amazing. She doesn't act like she has no legs. I don't mean she walks, but she's very independent. I liked her, but I like most females. Still, she's one of the nicest if not the nicest female I've met."

Izzy laughed and said, "What? I thought you liked me?"

"I do, but Grace is special. If you get to meet her, I think you'll agree."

139

The group continued talking as they entered the cabin.

Izzy went into the kitchen. "I've got a surprise for you, Pooh. Although, after you left without talking to us, I'm tempted to make you wait for it."

The weasel said, "I hope that P'Nut is okay. We learned that the woman Grace really is dangerous."

Annie said, "I thought you and P'Nut were enemies?"

"I suppose you could say that, but the little squirrel is a fighter and quite the duelist with a claw. I respect him, and, for now, we are on the same team. We need to recover the crystal."

Izzy returned, carrying a jar without a lid. It contained a beautiful, golden liquid. In her other hand, she held a big spoon. "Look what I have for you."

Pooh's nose informed him before he saw the jar. The little bear's eyes went wide. His stomach rumbled happily. He reached for the jar with both paws.

Izzy pointed the spoon at Pooh and pulled the jar back. "Now, Pooh, this jar needs to last."

Pooh could smell the wonderful fragrance of the honey. He didn't like waiting. "Oh, bother. Why don't you just give me the whole jar, please?"

"Silly, old bear."

The weasel said, "I think you should make him beg."

Annie said, "No, that wouldn't be nice."

The weasel said, "But it would be funny to watch."

Annie stuck the spoon into the jar. Carefully, she pulled the spoon out and twirled it to keep from losing any of the honey. "How do you want your honey, Pooh?"

"In my mouth." He opened his mouth wide and waited.

Izzy stuck the spoon in, and Pooh shut his mouth.

Weasel asked, "How is it?"

Pooh just said, "Mmmmm, mmmmm."

For a long time, Pooh just worked his tongue against the spoon and swallowed the liquid goodness. He hummed as he enjoyed the honey. Meanwhile, the weasel informed everyone about what he and Pooh had learned, including how the other bear might help them.

Annie said, "We should go after P'Nut to warn him."

Izzy said, "I don't think that will work. Remember, he told us to stay away from that area, and we agreed to."

Pooh couldn't get any more honey off the spoon, so, he spit it out. "We could go looking for the bear."

The weasel looked at Izzy. "What did you say?"

Izzy answered, "When we talked with P'Nut, we said we wouldn't go down toward the lake. So we could go explore up the rivers."

Annie walked over to the door and looked back at them. She looked happy to Pooh. Her big tongue hung out of the side of her mouth. Drool dripped from it.

Izzy walked over and opened the door. Everyone left the cabin. When they had gone into the cabin, all the shadows had been smaller. Now, they had started to grow again. Pooh looked at the sun and scratched his head. *The day is half over.*

Pooh remembered something else. "Did anyone get a chance to talk to the bat today?"

Izzy said, "No. I did check, and it's back in that small room. It's sleeping. So I left it alone. This evening, I'll try talking to it."

Pooh said, "Then we'll need to keep an eye on the time. We won't want to get back late."

Izzy laughed and Annie said, "Don't you just love her laughter."

The weasel said, "I've never thought about human laughter. It isn't something I do."

Izzy said, "Pooh, you aren't the only one that likes to eat. My stomach will help get us back in plenty of time. I have a good meal planned for tonight."

It didn't take them long to get to the bridge. Everyone stood on it and looked both directions. No one saw the bear.

Pooh said, "When we were here last, I saw a bird diving into the water. I think it or the other birds in the area might have an idea whether the bear is around."

Annie said, "That sounds like a good idea. I've seen other birds but not very many other animals around."

The weasel said, "We could split up. Half of us go up the river, and the other half go down to where the rivers join to make the bigger river."

Izzy said, "I don't like that idea. In all the mysteries and horror stories I know of, splitting up always leads to trouble."

Pooh said, "Okay. How about Annie and I go up the far side of the river and you two go up this side. This way, we can keep an eye on each other."

The weasel said, "Good idea. Let's get going. Pooh, if you see Grace, tell her 'hi' for me."

Pooh continued across the bridge with Annie. The pool of water had one fewer fish in it. The pool looked smaller. Pooh pointed and said, "See that pool? When we came back, there was one more fish in it. Something has been here and caught a fish out of this pool."

Annie ran ahead and squeezed through the alders beside the road. She ran on top of a log and jumped down onto the gravel surrounding the pool. Nose down to the ground, Annie smelled all around.

Pooh followed, but he moved slower and much more carefully. He remembered his fall into the pool. He didn't want to fall again. By the time he got down to the gravel, Annie had left the pool and started up the river toward some brush.

Annie said, "I found a trail. It was a raccoon. It dragged a fish this direction."

Pooh followed her. He caught the smell of a new animal. *That must be the raccoon.* Pooh also could smell the fish. He ran to catch up.

A voice came from under the bush. "That's close enough. Why are you two following me? There are more fish back in that pool. Go get your own."

Annie said, "We aren't after your fish. We're looking for a bear that lives here. Have you seen him?"

"I saw him yesterday. He was down here. He warned me about the flood yesterday. He said something about getting tired of watching out for Grace. He thinks she's getting worse. I think he's going to leave."

"Where is he?"

"You could try up higher on this river. He went that direction."

Pooh looked upstream. On the other side of the river, he saw Izzy climbing over some boulders.

Annie ran over and splashed into the edge of the river. "We just found out the bear is probably higher up on this river."

Izzy pointed upstream and said something, but Pooh couldn't hear her over the stream. By the time he reached the shore, Annie had raced on ahead. She disappeared over a small rise next to the stream.

A rock clattered down, surprising him. Pooh whirled. *What was that? Could it be the crazy donkey?* Pooh remembered his horrible dream about the crazy donkey. A feeling of ice crackled down his back, and he shuddered.

Pooh heard Annie say excitedly, "Rabbits, rabbits."

The little bear hurried up the small hill. On the other side, Annie ran around in a small meadow surrounded by trees. She chased after a rabbit until it disappeared. Another would appear farther away, and Annie would run after it.

Pooh said, "Oh, bother. Annie, what are you doing?"

"Chasing rabbits. It's fun."

"What would you do if you caught one?"

"I don't know. I suppose I would lick it and rub against it. Rabbits are cute."

Pooh shook his head. "I don't understand you. My paws are sore. I can't imagine running around just for fun. I want a snick-snack, preferably honey and a nap."

Annie asked, "What's a snick-snack?"

"Isn't it obvious? Snick-snack is a small amount of very enjoyable food. When I get peckish, I want a snick-snack."

"Peckish?"

"It's a bit hungry."

Annie said, "You have lots of unusual words for food."

Pooh said, "Food is important. Right now, we have something important to do. We need to keep going up the stream, looking for the bear, and not chasing rabbits."

Annie said, "I'm sorry." She ran over to Pooh and walked beside him.

Pooh placed a paw on Annie's back. It felt good. "Is it okay if I'm leaning a little on you?"

"Of course."

They crossed the meadow and walked up another hill under some pine trees. The pine needles felt good under Pooh's paws. At the top of the small hill, Pooh saw Izzy much farther ahead on the other side of the river.

On their side of the river, huge boulders lay jumbled up next to a twenty-foot rock cliff. Pooh said, "We're falling behind, and I don't know how we are going to get over these rocks."

Annie said, "Why don't you float? I can do the same thing. We could get past these rocks and catch up."

Pooh said, "Just a minute." He had smelled some plants which he knew would be very tasty. Following his nose, he found them at the base of some boulders. It only took him a minute to chomp down on the wonderful, juicy plants. Chewing on them, he noticed other plants that had been bitten off. He could smell another bear. It smelled fairly fresh.

He looked for Annie, finally spotting her hovering above the cliff. She gazed at something upriver. Pooh tried to talk with his mouth full. "Annie...I....Oh, ... bother."

Pooh floated up to her and swallowed. "I smelled the bear down there. He stopped to eat some of the same plants I just tasted."

Annie said, "Look upstream."

Ahead of them, Pooh spotted Izzy standing on a big boulder out in the middle of the river. It didn't look like she could get the rest of the way across without help. She just stood still and gazed at the hill above the river.

Pooh turned to look at the hill. At first, he didn't notice anything different. Then, it struck him. Trees covered the hills, but one big patch of the hillside on their side was treeless. "Annie, what is Izzy looking at?"

"The bear is up there, and it's a very strange hillside."

Pooh lifted his nose and smelled. Different smells drifted on the breeze that blew down the river valley. Pooh did recognize the bear, and deer smells, but there was another stronger smell. *What's that?* Then he remembered. "There are pikas up there."

"What are pikas?"

"They are little creatures that look like a cross between a rabbit and a mouse."

Movement on the hill drew Pooh's attention. A big tree on the edge of the clearing fell, but it didn't drop to the ground. Pooh gazed in shock. The tree had started to fall, but it stopped. The tree floated in air. The little bear watched in amazement as the tree drifted through the air to settle down gently by some others.

Pooh scratched his head. He drifted closer to see better. The closer he got, the better he saw the details. The bear stood by a tree just above the edge of the clearing. Two deer stood in the clearing just below the bear. *Dad told me bears eat deer. That bear is big. What's going on?* The treeless part of the hillside had a pattern to it. His curiosity grew. Pooh moved faster. He'd almost reached the edge of the clearing. From below came a loud whistle.

146

"Danger, danger from above."

Something shoved him hard. Pooh felt the wind knocked out of him. The little bear recognized it from the aerial battle he'd had at the camp. Reacting quickly, Pooh pushed himself to the side and up. Gasping, he caught his breath. The bear and the bucks stood by the upper edge of the clearing. The deer stood below the bear.

Pooh retreated from the clearing's border. The little bear soared around and up, staying back from the edge of the clearing. Pooh came in from above the clearing. "Mr. Bear, can I talk to you?"

In a deep voice, the bear answered, "Yes, if you want to stop flying around like an overgrown bird. Come in slowly, and land on the hill above me. The pikas won't be frightened by you, and I promise not to eat you."

Not to eat me? Pooh remembered his dad saying male bears would sometimes eat cubs. The closer he came, the bigger the other bear looked. Pooh landed slowly. He didn't want to embarrass himself by stumbling and falling, and the big bear made him very nervous.

When Pooh landed on his hind paws and looked at the big bear standing on all four paws and downhill from him, the big bear's eyes were on the same level as his. *He's really big.* "Hello, I'm Pooh. I'm looking for you. I mean I was looking for you. I... I mean we wanted to ask you something."

"You found me. What do you want?"

Many questions percolated in Pooh's mind. He didn't remember his mother at all. Since losing her, he'd never met another bear. Pooh didn't know what to ask first. *I can talk with another bear for the first time. What should I say? I don't want to appear stupid.*

One of the bucks said, "He said 'we.' Do you see anyone else with him?"

147

The other buck said, "No. I don't. Maybe he's crazy."

The first buck said, "Good, I thought I might be going blind. This cub said, 'We wanted to ask you something.'"

The big bear said, "Shut up, and let the cub think."

A buck said, "Yes. We can."

The other said, "You shouldn't have said anything. He wants us to be quiet."

"You're being less quiet than I am."

"No, I'm not."

The bear said, "Ignore them. They're smart in some ways, but very crazy in others. I smell human and dog smell on you. Why is that?"

Pooh had just started to ask about whether the big bear could help them get the crystal back from Grace. At the bear's words, Pooh's mind stopped working. Instead of what he'd planned to say, he just spoke from his heart. "You're the first bear I've seen since my mother died when I was a baby cub. Two humans raised me. They tried to teach me how to survive as a bear, but I have so many questions."

The little bear's mind started working again. "I'm sorry. I was looking for you with my friends. We're trying to get something from Grace that she took. It's very important. Can you help us?"

A buck said, "Wow, he's an orphan."

The other said, "Humans raised him. That's strange."

The big bear turned and growled at the two bucks. "If you're not going to shut up, go away."

"You can't hurt us. We're in the pikas' no-kill zone."

The big bear took a step toward them. "Kill? Who said anything about killing? I thought I'd just rip your hides open."

The bucks jumped and bounded away.

Pooh hurriedly took a couple of steps back from the big bear.

The bear turned back toward him. "You aren't starving. You'll learn what you don't know. Grace is trouble. She's tried to shoot me twice. I don't like her at all. I'm leaving. Even the pikas have had trouble with her. See the metal thing down by the river?"

Pooh saw sunlight reflecting from something. "Yes."

"Grace uses them. She sent one here. I think she wanted some of the pikas. Why, I don't know. With all the changes, I now have strange friends, but I still don't understand humans. I do respect the old man."

The big bear stopped speaking. He started walking away, but turned back to say one more thing. "Something else, cub, don't get the wrong idea. My world has changed. I've changed, but if I was hungry and ran into a lone cub like you, I might eat it."

Chapter Sixteen

P'Nut Finds More Danger

History is a funny thing. Kingdoms become republics, and the republics become empires ruled by an emperor. Religions about love, grace, help, and foregoing sin become bureaucratic organizations ruled by despotic sinners. Secret societies form to help society and free people, and ,then, they get used by governments to attack political enemies. Triads are some of those secret societies which are now no more than international criminal organizations.

Unfortunately, Triads and all other criminal organizations will continue to use any technological advancement for their own purposes. From 2018 through 2025, China was reported to be working on human and artificial intelligence (AI) interfaces to advance what would be android intelligence.

Bond said, "I am arranging a new pick up for you and the dog. Keep it safe until then. Do you know of any other animals or humans who can do strange things?"

P'Nut remembered the bear, Pooh. He hesitated to mention the silly bear. "Uh, there's this bear."

"What can he do?"

"Well, he can float up into the air."

Bond said, "That sounds like the dog. Protect the bear, too. I'll make sure the aircraft I send to pick you up can hold at least three passengers."

"Okay." P'Nut didn't know what else to say. *Pooh's important?*

Bond said, "I'm sending you some new gadgets. They should get there sometime today."

At that comment, a question popped into P'Nut's mind. "Where do you get the gadgets from?"

"I have a fabrication satellite. It makes what my agents need. A capsule carrying the gadgets brings those things down to my agents."

"Oh. Thanks." *Why did I even ask? I don't understand what he said.*

Bond said one more thing. "Whatever you do, stay away from the New Dragon Triad. They are extremely dangerous. They would love to turn you into an android."

A shiver of fear ran down P'Nut's back. "There is no way I'm getting close to them."

"Be careful. I will be in touch."

"Thanks. Bye."

P'Nut looked at the trees around him. The trunks and bushes kept him from seeing very far. *I better get back. I need to be sure the bear and the dog are safe.*

P'Nut scampered over the pine needles and pinecones under the trees. His ever-alert eyes spied some oval flat things on the ground. His nose identified a plump seed on the narrow end.

The little squirrel didn't know this food, but his nose told him it must be from the pine trees, and that it would be good. It only took him a second to pick it up and hold it in his front paws. P'Nut's sharp incisors made quick work of the seed. Quickly, he scouted about and found more. He nibbled on a low-hanging rose hip.

At an unusual sound, P'Nut froze with the red fruit of the rose at his mouth. Nothing moved around him. He stayed frozen for another second. The sound didn't repeat.

No longer interested in the rose hip, P'Nut dropped it. It had been dry and not very tasty, but, more importantly, the little squirrel remembered his need to get back to the others.

P'Nut ran along the side of the steep hill. Every now and then, he stopped. The little squirrel squatted on his haunches and looked carefully around.

He looked below. P'Nut couldn't see any of the robots or Grace. *I don't want to go back down too soon. Up here, I should be safe.*

P'Nut resumed running. P'Nut remembered the other squirrel. *He thought it was safe up here.*

Another noise froze P'Nut. *Something's coming.* The noise came from above. P'Nut relaxed. *It won't be the robots.* It grew louder and P'Nut leapt into a tree and raced up for a better vantage point.

From the higher location, P'Nut had a better view. He heard a sharp sound of something metallic hitting a rock. *What? It couldn't... I'm safe up here.* P'Nut ran out onto a branch. A shiver went down his back.

Bushes shook from back the way he'd come. A metallic form carrying a big animal strode out of the bushes. P'Nut recognized the animal as a mountain goat similar to the ones he'd seen up at Aneroid Lake. Another robot stepped out of the bushes. It carried a squirrel.

The squirrel looked exactly like the one P'Nut had talked to. P'Nut opened his mouth to scold the robots. Terror froze him with his mouth hanging open. *What am I thinking? They'll get me.*

152

P'Nut didn't know what to do. The hillside no longer represented a place of safety. A warning call from a bird unfroze him.

"Danger, danger. Look out for the hawk. Danger, danger. Look out for the hawk."

From above, a hawk dove at P'Nut. Its talons reached for the little squirrel perched on the branch.

P'Nut jumped and vibrated immediately. The hawk's talons passed through the little squirrel.

The hawk screamed, as it slammed against the branch. "What!? Where did he go!?"

P'Nut kept vibrating. He flipped over the hawk and down through the branches of the tree. The little squirrel stopped vibrating to land on a branch. P'Nut wasn't vibrating, but he shook from the end of his nose to the end of his tail. Branches blocked his view, but he heard the robots.

"Don't shoot the hawk. We can't recover it from the tree. Keep moving. Grace wants these animals. We need them ready to ship out. There's another flight coming in tonight."

P'Nut heard the noise of the machines descending the slope. His heart threatened to pound out of his chest. His tail shivered over his back.

The birds who'd warned him harassed the hawk. "Leave our area. Leave our area. Don't come back."

The hawk replied, "If you'll leave me alone, I'll gladly fly away."

P'Nut shifted his weight from paw to paw. His mouth hung open, and he panted in terror. His fear rattled thoughts around in his head. Are the robots gone? *When are my new gadgets coming? I hope there's something to use against these robots. I thought it was safe up here. Where can I find safety? I need to go back up to Aneroid*

Lake.

Finally, P'Nut couldn't stand still anymore. He ran from branch to branch and leapt across the gaps between the trees. P'Nut leapt over a ravine and landed on another branch. The little squirrel ran along it toward the tree trunk. His always-busy eyes spotted a moth caught in a web. P'Nut shuddered as he saw the spider approaching. *I'm just like that moth, except I'm not caught in a web. I'm caught in my fear.* P'Nut looked around. He couldn't hear any robots. *I can't let my fear control me.* He remembered the big man on the plane. P'Nut remembered how he copied the TV psychologist to help the man. *I helped him deal with the fear of his past. I need help. This terror is too much for me.*

P'Nut looked down the ravine. *My friends are down there. I'm supposed to save the dog, Annie, and the others, especially that silly bear, need me, but I'm just a little squirrel. I'm no hero.*

I helped the man see the past differently and to look past it. I need to go back down. My friends are down there. They are counting on me. I'm terrified, but they are in danger, too. I need to let them know what has happened. We should move back up the mountain.

P'Nut carefully looked both up the steep slope and down. Nothing moved. *It's too quiet. It's so hot.*

The little squirrel jumped down into the ravine. Moving fast, he descended. P'Nut didn't stop to look. He didn't stop to listen. He just moved fast. At times, he leapt back into the trees and raced through the branches. *I'm getting too hot.* The scene with the gorilla played over in his mind. Again, P'Nut saw the two robots descending from above. A dread grew in the little squirrel. *I need help. I can't do this on my own. What will I find at the cabin?*

The ground leveled out. P'Nut raced up a tree and looked. He saw the strange poles holding the wires above them. He looked down toward the lake. The road seemed quiet. *If the robots are hunting up on the mountain, they'll be coming this way.*

P'Nut squinted, trying to see more clearly. His mouth hung open. His breath came hard and fast. *I need to rest for a moment.* P'Nut raced back down the tree, leapt down, and dashed under a bush. He lay down flat on a cool, white and black speckled boulder. P'Nut stretched his legs out flat against the boulder. He felt the coolness easing into him and the heat flowing away. P'Nut splooted against the rock.

He lay there as long as he dared. It felt so good. *I've got to go.* P'Nut raced through the grass and dashed up one of the poles. He raced on the wires. It didn't take him long to reach the next pole. *I'm going too slowly.*

Ahead of him and to his right, P'Nut saw the bridge. A strange sight met his eyes. The little squirrel stopped on the wire. His tail flipped back and forth. On the other side of the river, a small donkey, his head hanging low, plodded along a road.

What is it doing? Where did it come from? P'Nut looked ahead toward where he knew the cabin stood in the trees. *My friends should be there. I need to get them to safety.* P'Nut raced to the next pole. He leapt to it and sped headfirst down it. Without pausing, the little squirrel dashed across the road.

The donkey had reached the bridge and started across. P'Nut raced to another pole, leapt up onto it and looked around. The plodding of the donkey's hooves echoed in the still air. *Crazy animal. That noise is going to attract robots.* The steady beats blended with the sounds of the river. P'Nut looked around. For the moment, it seemed to be safe. *I need to get it to be quiet.*

P'Nut said, "Hello, I'm P'Nut. Who are you?"

The donkey plodded on toward him. "My name is Eeyore. I need help, but I probably won't find any."

P'Nut ran around on the pole. *Of course, he needs help. All of us*

155

need help. This— Wait, maybe he knows something. "Why do you need help? Why do..."

The donkey said, "I've lost my home in a storm. I'm trying to find a new home, but each home I've found either falls down or is in a dangerous location. I shouldn't expect to find any help, but I need to keep trying."

During the donkey's explanation, P'Nut ran up higher on the pole to check out the area and, then, ran back down. *I don't see any threats.* He ran around the pole three times, looking. At the donkey's conclusion, P'Nut stopped running. "You're right. You should always keep trying. You can come with me. Our cabin is about as safe as anything around here."

"Okay. I might as well. It can't be worse than anywhere I've been, although it probably will be."

P'Nut said, "My name is P'Nut. What's your name?"

The donkey plodded on. His hoofbeats echoed. "I'm Eeyore. I probably shouldn't stay with you. I have very bad luck. I caused the others to die."

P'Nut said, "I don't plan on dying. I'm going to save my friends. We need to leave. Can you get off the road? Your hooves make lots of noise. I'm worried the robots will hear you."

Eeyore answered. "I can get off the road. I'm sorry I'm so noisy. You're right. Maybe it would be better if I didn't follow you. I wouldn't want to attract the robots to you."

The little squirrel ran off the road and into the trees. "Follow me." *This donkey is crazy.* P'Nut raced ahead, leapt onto a tree and looked back. Eeyore plodded steadily after him. Under the trees, the pine needles and pinecones muffled his hoofbeats.

P'Nut realized he could hardly catch his breath. *How far have I run?* The little squirrel rested as the donkey slowly plodded between the trees.

Eeyore said, "Someone is coming."

What? P'Nut raced up the tree until he could see through the branches. The tall skinny girl ran up the road. He looked at Eeyore. "Get over here and lie down."

The donkey plodded over to him. "Why?"

"I'm hoping that girl hasn't seen you. Lie down and be quiet. When she runs past us, I'll follow her. You stay still."

Eeyore slowly slumped down onto his side. "I don't know why you are fussing over me so much. I'm bad luck. It's probably my fault this girl you are worried about is coming."

P'Nut looked at Eeyore in exasperation. "What is wrong with you? This isn't your fault. Now, be quiet."

Eeyore said, "I caused my friends to die." He paused before adding, "I caused my mom's death."

P'Nut carefully watched the approach of the girl. She had stopped running and walked up the road. They had time. *What is this crazy donkey talking about? Why isn't he being quiet?* "Keep your voice down. How did you cause their deaths?"

"I thought you wanted me to be quiet?"

The little secret agent looked at the donkey. He looked back at the laborious progress of the skinny girl. *She's not even walking very fast. What's she doing?* P'Nut looked back at Eeyore. "Speak quietly. We have time. The girl's moving very slowly. Please, tell me how you caused their deaths, but speak quietly."

The words poured out of the little donkey. P'Nut felt the pain seasoning the words. "When I was a foal, there was a storm. I wanted to go out and run in the wind and rain. The others tried to call me back into the barn, but I was having too much fun. Having fun was bad. They all came out into the storm. They were too close to a big, tall tree. Lightning hit the tree. It killed them.... My mom lived the longest. She made me promise not to give up and to keep on living."

P'Nut gazed at the donkey in shock. *That's horrible. Is everyone crazy?* He remembered talking to and helping the big man on the plane. *What do I say? What would the TV psychologist say?* "First, their deaths were not your fault. You were young. It was their responsibility to teach you what's safe. They made the choice to come out into the storm, and it was their bad luck to be close to the tree."

Eeyore opened his mouth to reply but shut it.

Inspiration hit P'Nut. He remembered something his old friends had said. He asked, "Eeyore, are you living life?"

"What do you mean? I'm trying not to die."

"Exactly, these trees around us are trying not to die, but they aren't living life. They are just plants, but you and me, we have choices. We can choose to just respond to events and try not to die, or we can make hard choices to truly live. That means doing things when you're frightened instead of running away, and it means helping others, but most importantly, it means enjoying life."

Eeyore stared at him. The sound of shoes hitting the ground pulled P'Nut's attention away. The girl had started running again, and she ran right toward them. Quietly, he said, "Stay here. Be quiet. I'm going to go talk to her."

P'Nut jumped up and ran over to the edge of the road.

The girl ran toward him. Her face was red. Tears ran down it. She gasped out words. They hit P'Nut like gasoline on a fire. Terror was his fire. "You... should... have... left.... Grace... is... preparing... to... capture... all... of... you.... You need... to go."

P'Nut's thoughts swirled. His eyes lifted to the sky. *I've to get the others. Where are my new gadgets? I shouldn't have worried*

158

about—

Eeyore's voice interrupted his swirling thoughts. "Just like I expected, my bad luck is affecting you."

P'Nut spun. The donkey stood over him. The little squirrel looked up and spat out words. "Enough, enough, you stupid donkey. This was happening with or without you. Don't you get it? Bad stuff happens. I'm not letting this bad stuff hurt my friends." At those words, P'Nut's thoughts crystallized into action. He looked back at the girl. "Come to the cabin." He turned away, not waiting for her answer.

"I can't. Grace will kill me. I have to go back."

The little squirrel turned back to her, leapt forward, grabbed the bottom of her jeans, and tugged. He yelled. "What is it with everyone? Living in fear is not living. It is letting fear live your life for you. I will not let fear live my life. My life is my own. My life is my own. Yes, I'm afraid. I'm terrified, but fear won't live my life."

P'Nut ordered, "You two, follow me to the cabin."

He turned around and ran. *I'll get everyone else. I will get them to safety.*

Chapter Seventeen

Sweet Grace is Captured

Being able to control gravity would be a game changer. How would you like to fly through the air? The ability to control gravity would affect all of life. Moving things would become much, much easier. Unfortunately, controlling gravity would probably get used in some way as a weapon. Very powerful people would do anything to gain that power.

Pooh and Annie landed on the other side of the river. Pooh told Izzy and the weasel, "I talked to the bear. He isn't going to help. Maybe we should give up trying to get the crystal. P'Nut said that Annie is important. We shouldn't risk her getting captured by this horrible person."

Izzy said, "We shouldn't give up without thinking about it. It's getting late. Let's go back to the cabin and talk to P'Nut. He's the secret agent. He'll know what's best. Maybe he learned something today. He'll know what to do."

Pooh shrugged. "Okay."

Together they slowly made their way back down the river. Pooh alternated between floating over obstacles and walking in the easier stretches. A tantalizing smell caught his attention. His stomach growled. "Go on ahead. I'll catch up. I need to eat some more."

Annie said, "Pooh, you eat all the time."

Pooh said, "I'm still just a cub. I need to eat a lot. My parents told me that during late summer and fall, I'll eat much more than normal. This is what I need to do."

Annie said, "Okay."

Izzy said, "Okay, Pooh, but don't get so busy eating that you forget to come. Remember, I'm fixing a great dinner."

Pooh hardly heard her. He absentmindedly said, "Okay." He let his nose lead him. He drifted down between some boulders to a secluded and shady spot. His nose told him of a great amount of wonderful food just ahead. A thought drifted like smoke through his mind. *I'll get back to the cabin in time for her dinner, but first....*

~**********~

Annie jumped into a pool of water and splashed joyfully through it. "Izzy, you should jump into the water. It's wonderful, and it will cool you off."

Izzy said, "The sun is already going behind the ridge. It's going to start cooling off. I think I'll just climb around."

"Okay. Suit yourself, but the water isn't deep. I wouldn't invite you in if I thought you could drown."

The weasel said, "Annie, I think you should be lifting us through the air."

Annie asked, "Are we in a hurry? We'll still beat Pooh back to the cabin."

"Not if Pooh takes the easy way back by floating. It has been a while since we left the hungry bear."

Annie hated the idea of leaving the stream. It felt so good to jump into each pool of water they came to. An inspiration came to her. She waded out into the deepest part of the pool and lifted herself and a bubble of water into the air.

She heard Izzy laugh. The happy dog said, "You like my new idea? I'm a good dog? Do you want to float with part of your body in a bubble of water like I am?"

Izzy laughed again and said, "No, thank you, but I agree about moving faster. That will give me time to take a rest before fixing dinner. I'm still a bit worn out from yesterday."

A boom echoed from the sky. Annie looked up trying to spot the source of the noise. "What was that?"

The weasel answered, "I think your friend, P'Nut, is getting some new gadgets. I hope they're worth the noise. We better hurry back."

Annie used gravity to lift Izzy and her passenger, the weasel, into the air. With a pang, she remembered what had happened at the lake. "Oh, Izzy, how can you trust me to lift you through the air. I drowned you at the lake."

Izzy firmly answered, "Now, Annie, we've talked about that. I do trust you. You are a good dog. You succeeded in carrying us away from our enemies. At the lake, you still did your best." She ended with three very firm words. "I trust you."

Annie wagged her tail. "Okay."

Together, the friends and the weasel floated back down the stream. It didn't take long until the bridge came into view. Annie turned their course toward the cabin.

Izzy spoke up, "Annie, do you see something on that boulder below the bridge?"

Annie changed their course and gently dropped them lower. She scanned the river looking for what Izzy had seen. Annie spotted the boulder and what lay on it, at the same time, as Izzy spoke again.

"Annie, there's a bird on that boulder. I think it's a camp robber."

The weasel said, "It's a jay." In a much more concerned and softer tone he added, "A camp robber watched over Grace."

Izzy asked, "Grace?"

The weasel said, very impatiently, "Get me closer. Hello. Are you okay?"

The bird on the boulder did not look okay to Annie. In fact, she looked dead, but she didn't smell dead.

The bird answered, but her voice didn't carry clearly over the river's noise.

Annie dropped them lower. "What did you say?"

The bird lifted her head and spoke again, and, this time, her words could be understood. "Grace has been taken by a robot. I tried to fight it off, but it almost killed me. I tried to fly for help. Please, save Grace. If you hurry, you'll catch the robot before it takes her down to the lodge. They're on the right side of the river. Hurry. Don't let it take Grace to the lodge. They do horrible things in the lodge."

The bird dropped her head and lay still.

Annie said, "We need to help this poor bird."

The weasel shouted, "Didn't you hear what she said!? We have to go rescue Grace. We don't have much time."

Izzy asked, "Grace is the little girl you and Pooh told us about?"

"Yes. Annie, take us down the river, but up higher so we can spot the robot carrying Grace."

Annie started to lift them higher. Izzy said, "First, we should tell Pooh and especially P'Nut what we are doing."

Annie could see the cabin they used. In the other direction, a scintillating flash of light off moving metal caught her attention. *The robot.*

The weasel said, "Didn't you listen. There isn't time. We have to go, right now."

Another noise—not the noise of the river below but a noise from above—turned Annie's attention from the argument. It was a familiar noise. Her tail wagged in hope of what the noise signaled. Annie paused their ascent into the sky, and she looked for the source of the noise. A very small rapidly approaching dot rewarded her search.

A brash, excited voice preceded the rapidly enlarging dot. "Hello, Annie. Hello, Izzy. I found you."

An exclamation gave voice to Izzy's emotions, "What?"

The weasel just asked, "Who is that?"

Annie joyously gave voice to her feelings. "Fuego. Fuego. Fuego."

"Yes. It is I. The valiant hero is flying again. It's good to find you."

The weasel said, "We don't have time for a reunion. We need to go save sweet Grace."

"Is there a battle? Where? Let's go. Oh, I forgot. I can no longer create fireballs."

Izzy pointed at their cabin. She spoke very quickly. "Fuego, I'm so glad you're okay. You came just in time. Go to that cabin. Our friend, the secret agent, P'Nut, will hopefully be there. He's a squirrel. Let him know we are going toward the lake to rescue a little girl from a robot." She paused and added. "After you go to the cabin, come back to this river and go upstream. Look for a bear cub wearing a red shirt. He's Pooh and a friend of ours. Let him know what we are doing. We better go. Thanks. Bye."

Annie took one last, happy look at her friend, Fuego, humming off to P'Nut. Then, she turned to the task of rescuing the little girl.

~**********~

P'Nut twirled around to face Eeyore and the tall girl. "Come on. We have to move faster."

Eeyore plodded faster, but the tall girl gasped, "I'm sorry. I can't go faster."

The little squirrel jumped up onto a pole and looked back toward the lake. "I don't see anyone coming. Get off the road and walk through the woods. Eeyore, come with the girl to the cabin. Stay out of sight of the road and be quiet."

P'Nut jumped down and raced ahead. "I'll go get my friends. Together, we'll escape." A boomed echoed from the sky. P'Nut looked up. *My new gadgets. I'll need those to help us.*

Eeyore said, "That noise attracted attention."

P'Nut muttered, "Yeah, but it'll be worth it." *I hope.* He jumped onto the porch and with another jump went through the door. "Hello."

Only the silence of the house answered him. *Where are they? They couldn't have gone toward the lake. I would've seen them. We agreed that they wouldn't go that direction.* P'Nut raced through the house looking for the others. *They aren't here.*

P'Nut jumped back through the door. Passing through it, he saw Eeyore and the skinny girl stepping onto the porch. Both of them screamed.

"Ahhh! Ahhh!"

"What!?" The girl jumped off the porch.

P'Nut landed on Eeyore's head. The startled donkey reared and jerked his head up. That sent P'Nut somersaulting over the donkey.

The little squirrel flipped through the air. He landed in time to see Eeyore twirl surprisingly fast for a fat little donkey.

The girl asked, "What did you just do?"

Eeyore agreed. "Yes. That scared me. Did you do that on purpose?"

P'Nut said, "Sorry. I can vibrate through solid objects."

"Oh."

Eeyore said, "Really? I didn't know anyone could do something like that."

P'Nut said, "My friends aren't here. Both of you go into the woods behind the house. Stay hidden and watch the road and the cabin. If you see robots or Grace coming, run away." He looked at the tall girl. "Do you know where the trail to Aneroid is?"

"Yes."

"Good, if the bad folks come, take Eeyore up that trail to safety. I'm going to get my new gadgets. I'll be right back."

P'Nut ran toward the road. He jumped up onto a pole and ran up to its top. From there he looked down to the lake and all around. Everything looked quiet, too quiet. *Where are my gadgets?*

Bond's voice interrupted his searching. "P'Nut, your new gadgets are landing across the road from the cabin you have been staying in.

Get over there and get them quickly. I am afraid their arrival has attracted attention."

P'Nut jumped onto a wire running from the pole to another on the other side of the road. *I'm moving slower. I need rest and food, but there's no time. Maybe the arrival of my gadgets will attract my friends' attention. I hope they are on the way back.*

~**********~

Pooh happily munched away on the wonderful variety of tasty plants. He'd even found some late berries. A loud boom interrupted his enjoyment. *What was that?* Pooh looked around. The shadows looked longer than he thought they should. *How long have I been eating?* Pooh looked at the shadows, but there weren't any shadows. He looked for the sun. Pooh couldn't see it. He looked at the right hand ridge. A shadow lay high against the ridge. *The sun's going down. I better get going. I hope I'm not late.*

With one last longing look, Pooh left the secluded plant buffet. He scrambled up a boulder and tumbled down the backside of it. Pooh landed with a splash in a small pool of water on the edge of the stream. He quickly looked around for any observers.

I should try floating. I wouldn't like to miss dinner. Pooh's stomach gurgled its agreement. This time Pooh didn't have to think about how the fish floated. He lifted gently off the ground and drifted down the stream. *I could go higher and maybe see if the others have already reached the cabin.* A different thought, cold and sharp, drove him closer to the stream. *If I go to high, a robot might see me. But the worst danger would be getting spotted by the crazy donkey.*

At the thought of the crazy donkey, Pooh not only dropped lower, but he also picked up his speed. Pooh skimmed just above the tops of the boulders. A paw brushed the top of a rock. *It wouldn't be good to hit a boulder and go tumbling. I should slow down.* A new worry had grown roots in his thoughts. Pooh had remembered his terrifying experience with the robot in the night. *Are my friends okay? Has that secret agent gotten back safely? That loud noise will attract the robots. Pooh flew faster over the boulders.*

~**********~

At that moment, P'Nut watched a new flying platform swoop in and hover in front of him. It hummed. *Cool. This one is so much bigger.* It had a similar place for him to ride, but there wasn't any screen. The open end of a bell shaped device pointed forward from the front.

P'Nut jumped on and scampered over to his seat. *How will I learn how to use it without a screen?* The platform shifted as his weight moved across it. *I wonder how much weight this can carry. It's about as long as a car.*

He settled into his seat and felt it strap him in. In front of him, a moving image flickered on in the air. *Now, we'll be okay. If any robots come, I'll be able to defend my friends. We can wait for the pickup.* At that thought, P'Nut remembered the last time Bond had planned to take him and the others to safety. It had been a vehicle flying through the air. *Can Bond make a pickup fly?* .Unfortunately, the previous craft had exploded in the sky.

Bond's voice came from the image. "Hello, P'Nut. This is much bigger than your last platform. It works the same way for flying."

At those words, P'Nut grasped the two handles and maneuvered the platform toward the road and the cabin on the other side of the road.

P'Nut listened to instructions and watched the holograph. The road was quiet. He darted across.

Bond's voice talked about the bell shaped device, and how it could be used against robots. Over the hum of the platform and the sound of Bond's voice, P'Nut heard another sharper humming. It was almost a buzzing sound.

Startled by the noise, P'Nut looked around. When he looked up, the cause of the sound zoomed down at him. *It's a hummingbird.*

The bird stopped in front of him. "Hello. I'm Fuego. Are you P'Nut?"

The little, three-inch-long creature didn't seem to be bothered in the least by P'Nut's newest gadget. That bothered the little squirrel. "Yes, I'm P'Nut." Then, he remembered where he'd heard the name, Fuego. *This is the heroic person who gave his life to save Annie and Izzy, except he didn't die.*

The hummingbird said, "Good. Annie and Izzy sent you a message. They are going to rescue a little girl."

"What?" *This is terrible news.*

"The girl has been captured by a robot."

"Where are they?"

"They've headed toward the lake."

P'Nut remembered the horror and terror that existed down by the lake. "No!" He only thought of only one possible plan. "Fuego, go behind the cabin down this lane. There is a donkey and a girl. Tell them what you told me and I'm going to help my friends. Tell them to stay safe."

Without another word, P'Nut turned his new flying platform toward the lake and took off down the road. *Will I get to Annie and Izzy in time to save them? This is crazy.*

Chapter Eighteen

A Rescue

Electromagnetic pulse (EMP) is a brief burst of electromagnetic disturbance. These pulses can disrupt communications and damage or even destroy electronic equipment.

EMPs can be caused naturally, such as by a solar storm. The worst EMP event in our history was the solar storm of August 1859. It was called the Carrington Event. When that event happened, it disrupted the telegraph systems of the day and caused the telegraph equipment to spark and caused some fires from the sparks.

Geological history shows that much worse events happen. Any one of those would devastate the technology and economy of our present world. Nuclear weapons also create EMPs. Those weapon created EMPs have a localized effect.

There are also smaller devices capable of creating EMPs. One of those could potentially disable robots.

Annie took them down the river. Immediately, she spotted the robot. It carried the little girl, Grace, in its arms. The robot walked along the road. Just ahead of the robot was an intersection. "Izzy, what should I do"

Izzy must've already been giving the problem some thought. She had an answer ready. "Can you use gravity to tear its head off like you tore apart the jet?"

Annie considered the question. It would be hard. "I can do it."

"Good. Set me down in front of the robot. Dump the water you are carrying with you on it, and then rip off its head."

"Okay."

They had almost reached the lake. In some trees ahead of them, Annie could see a building. Annie thought she saw movement around the building. "We'll have to hurry."

Annie obeyed. She dropped Izzy down in front of the robot

The robot stopped. Annie dropped the water on it. The robot managed to say, "What?"

Annie ripped its head off. The robot started to fall. Annie supported the destroyed robot until Izzy took the unconscious Grace from the robots arms.

Izzy said, "I've got her. Let's get out of here."

~**********~

P'Nut raced down the road toward the lake. Ahead of him, he saw where the gorilla had died. His paws tightened on the controls. A shiver travelled through his body. Terror threatened P'Nut's resolve to help his friends. He pushed the platform to move faster.

The platform tilted and side-slipped going around the turn. Annie and Izzy stood on the road ahead of him. *What are they doing? What's on the ground?* Ahead and all to close, P'Nut could see the lake. *Where are the robots?*

A damaged robot lay on the ground. Izzy held the body of a little girl. The girl had no legs. *I hope the little girl is okay. I'm glad they rescued the girl.* P'Nut relaxed his grip on the controls. *Now, I need to get them back to the cabin. I hope that silly bear Pooh is staying out of trouble.*

~**********~

Pooh followed the playful splashes and flow of the river until he saw the bridge. At a memory, his stomach rumbled. The little bear rose higher until he could see the small pool of water to the side of the stream. The fish still swam in the pool. Pooh remembered the taste of the fish. His stomach rumbled.

"No. Izzy is making dinner for us." Pooh swerved the other direction and left the river behind. In front of him, Pooh glimpsed something about the length of a car flying toward the lake. *What?*

Pooh hesitated. He wanted to check out the strange flying thing, but the idea of Izzy making dinner and expecting him won out. His stomach gurgled agreeably.

The idea of a dinner waiting made Pooh take a shortcut, He soared up and over the trees between him and the cabin. A humming sound drew his attention to some trees behind the house. Swinging around the tree tops and dropping in low to investigate, Pooh glimpsed something gray on the ground.

Pooh would've dropped down to investigate, but a humming sound rose and something small darted up to him. It slowed and stopped.

The little bear recognized the flying creature as a hummingbird.

The tiny bird stopped right in front of Pooh's nose. The bear had to look cross-eyed to see it.

The hummingbird said, "You must be Pooh. I'm Fuego. P'Nut has gone to help Annie and Izzy. They are rescuing a little girl."

The hummingbird hovered inches from Pooh's nose. The little bear knew of only one little girl. It had to be sweet, little Grace. "What can I do?"

Fuego drifted backward, "I don't know what you can do. I will take my sword and go help them."

Pooh looked at the tiny bird in confusion. "What sword? I don't see any sword."

Fuego buzzed right up and poked Pooh's nose with his beak. "Don't you see my mighty sword? Do you feel it?"

"Do you mean your beak?"

"Yes. It's my beak. Isn't it obvious? It should be. It's almost touching your useless nose."

Pooh backed up trying to see the tiny creature's beak. The beak could only be about a half-inch long. "Oh, it's a bit small for a sword."

Fuego flew even closer to Pooh's nose "My sword may be small. I may be small, but they will learn to fear me."

Pooh didn't know what to say to the intrepid little bird. He had all to clear a memory of the frightening robot. This bird would stand no chance against one of them. Pooh had heard of this hummingbird. Annie and Izzy had thought it had died. He was glad that they had been wrong. "You are definitely mighty, but I don't think your sword will do much against the robots. Izzy and Annie talked about you. Can't you do something with fireballs?"

Fuego answered, "Before my brush with death, I was a fearsome pyro-hummingbird. Unfortunately, after my life was saved, I no longer can create fireballs. It must be a temporary problem."

From below came a question, "Who's the bear?"

Someone answered, and Pooh thought it sounded like the tall girl. "He's one of those staying in this cabin."

The other voice asked, "Can he help us stay safe?"

Pooh spoke to Fuego, "I don't see how you can help."

"Enough of this talk. My friends need my help. Goodbye." The fearless, hummingbird buzzed away. The little bird disappeared toward the lake.

Pooh shook his head. *That bird is crazy. How can it help Izzy and Annie?*

~**********~

Annie looked at the limp, little girl lying in Izzy's arms. Annie wanted to drop down and lick her face. Licking always helped, if people let her lick them.

The weasel said, "I think we should get out of here."

The weasel's words made Annie stop gazing at the little girl. She looked up. Metal objects moved in the trees. "Uh, oh. I think we have company."

The weasel said, "Do your fancy work with gravity and lift us up. We need to leave."

Izzy said, "There's something coming toward us from the other direction. It looks bigger than the flying platform P'Nut used to fight the drones."

174

Annie couldn't decide what to do first. At Izzy's words, Annie spun in the air. "It's P'Nut. He's riding on it. Our secret agent will know what to do. We're going to be okay."

Izzy said, "I'm getting off this road."

~**********~

P'Nut didn't know what to do. Izzy ran toward him, carrying the little girl, and Annie floated above them. *The dog should get them all out of here, with her gravity ability, as fast as she can.* As he watched, the group angled off the road. "Bond, if you can hear me, I need some help. The instruction video is going too slowly. I understand the EMP weapon, but that sounds like a last resort."

Bond responded. "My sensors show multiple robots moving behind you. Get away from the road and closer to the river."

At those words, P'Nut glanced to his right. He spotted at least one robot moving down from the mountain. Quickly, P'Nut swerved off the road and between buildings. He dropped closer to the ground and swerved trying to take advantage of anything to block the robots from seeing him.

Bond's voice continued, "I believe they also have an EMP weapon. It would take out your new flying platform. Help is coming, but I am afraid it will be too late. Get the dog down out of the air. The robots will see the dog and tranquilize it. You do not want to get caught. What they are doing to animals is terrible."

P'Nut turned, tipped, and accelerated toward Annie. The dog looked confused. She turned back and forth.

Bond said, "Retreat into the woods across the river is your best option. Is there any hope that the bear you mentioned can help?"

"Annie, drop down close to the ground. There are robots behind us and over by the hill. We need to get down by the ground onto the other side of the river."

The dog obeyed. She dropped. Even as Annie maneuvered, P'Nut saw something fly past her. He turned to follow her and looked down. A couple of robots back by the road had long things pointed at them. P'Nut heard something hit the bottom of his platform. The horrible image of the gorilla filled the little squirrels mind. He screamed. "They're shooting at us! Get to the other side of the river."

P'Nut dove down into the edges of a tree's branches. The underside of his platform scrapped past them. P'Nut saw Annie lift Izzy to the other side of the river. *They're getting away. I can protect them.*

The little squirrel finally answered Bond about the bear. "I hope the bear stays away. He's nice, but he's clumsy and thinks too slowly."

~**********~

Pooh watched the hummingbird fly away. *What should I do?*

The voice Pooh didn't recognize said, "You shouldn't stay up there. One of the robots might see you. Not that it matters, we're probably doomed anyway."

Pooh dropped down to the ground and landed on his hind paws. "Hello, I'm Pooh."

"I'm Eeyore. I'm probably going to bring you bad luck."

Pooh looked at the tall girl. He expected she would introduce herself, but she kept looking out at the road and then uphill toward the trail to Aneroid Lake.

Instead of introducing herself, she said, "I think we should go up the trail to the lake. The squirrel told me that would be a place of safety."

Pooh liked the sound of that, but he looked down the hill toward the other lake. *My friends are down there. I promised to help them.* "You two, take the trail to safety. Tell any animal you meet that Pooh sent you to Owl. Tell Owl what is happening. Keep Eeyore safe. I'm going to help my friends."

The girl said, "Come on, Eeyore."

~**********~

Eeyore looked between Pooh and the girl. New ideas, old ideas, and his old attitude warred inside the little donkey. Slowly, carefully, he spoke. "If I go with you, trouble might follow us up to this other lake." He looked at Pooh. "Pooh, I've never had a friend. Would you be my friend?"

Pooh looked at the strange creature. With his droopy ears, Eeyore looked sad and in need of a friend. "Yes, Eeyore. I'll be your friend."

"Good. Thank you. I'm going to stay with you, Pooh, and I'll try to be a good friend."

The tall girl backed away from them. "I'm sorry. I should stay and try to help, but I just can't. I'll go to Owl and pass on what's happening."

Eeyore said, "You brought the warning. That took courage. Thank you."

Tears started running down the girl's face. She whispered, "Thank you." Turning around, she hurried through the trees.

177

Eeyore looked at Pooh. "I've heard friends help friends. What can I do to help?" The little bear didn't answer. Eeyore added, "I've heard that bad things just happen, but I should warn you bad things happen around me. I hope I'm not really bad luck."

Pooh stepped up to Eeyore and put a paw up on his back. "At one time, I thought I was bad luck. My mother died when I was a baby cub. I thought I might have been the cause."

Eeyore lifted his head. "My mother died too. Ever since, I've thought I was the cause. It's made it hard to live."

Pooh said, "My foster parents helped me. They told me it wasn't my fault. They helped me."

Eeyore said, "They sound nice. I didn't have anyone to help me." He remembered the mouse. "There were some that wanted to help, but I didn't listen to them. I'm going to listen to you. What should we do?"

Pooh spoke with a confidence Eeyore had never heard before or even imagined. "We are going to go help our friends."

~**********~

P'Nut dove his craft across the river. A ping told him of robots still shooting at him.

Movement on the ground caught P'Nut's attention. The weasel had jumped off Izzy. The little creature dashed from boulder to boulder. He paused and dashed under a bush. All the time, he headed downstream.

P'Nut looked up just in time to see Izzy fall to the ground. Annie must've seen her fall. Izzy and the little girl's limp bodies lifted off the ground and up between the trees.

The little squirrel almost panicked at seeing Izzy get hit. P'Nut swerved his flying platform more violently and succeeded on diving into the trees without hearing any more pings and more importantly, without getting hit himself and falling unconscious.

Secluded in the trees, Annie stopped, and for a moment they were safe. "What are we going to do?"

Annie hovered above the ground below her, the little girl and Izzy lay limply on the ground.

Bond's voice saved P'Nut from trying to figure out what to do. "Have the dog move through the trees and go up the hill. It will be steep, but that will work to her benefit."

P'Nut said, "Take Izzy and the little girl farther into these trees. Stay low to the ground, and watch out for robots. Try to get to the hill ahead of us and go up it."

"Okay. What will you do?"

He answered in as determined a voice as he could muster. His determination had fought a losing fight against the terrible memory of the gorilla. P'Nut tried to keep the terror out of his voice. "I'll distract them."

P'Nut lifted above the trees. At first, he moved slowly, but he quickly picked up speed.

Bond said, "Remember, they have an EMP weapon. Don't stay out in the open or they'll disable the aerial mobility unit."

At those words, P'Nut dove back down to the tree tops. In the dive he spotted two drones leaving the lodge by the lake. They didn't come after him. *They're after Annie and Izzy.*

His new flying platform had small missiles. P'Nut readied a clawed finger on the trigger for them.

Dodging around trees, P'Nut sped after them. Somehow, the

devices knew his purpose. They picked up speed. Soon the three raced down roads amongst the trees. At one tree, one drone went left and the other right around the tree.

P'Nut spotted Annie and Izzy to the left. He went left. The drone swerved toward his friends. P'Nut side-slipped, fired, and the drone blew up.

He spun into a hammerhead turn. His instinct had been right. The other drone flew right at him. He flipped the front of his platform up as he heard a ping from the bottom of his craft.

P'Nut crouched down to give the drone a smaller target and flipped level. P'Nut fired as the drone dodged left. The drone sped around the same tree it had just come around. The missile P'Nut had fired sped after it. It hit the tree and exploded.

P'Nut followed the drone. He sped as fast as he dared. His platform slew to the left.

The drone had sped up too. It slew farther to the left. P'Nut followed in hot pursuit, trying to get back into a firing configuration.

His speed kept him slewing too far to the left. He couldn't get lined up unless he slowed down. *If I slow down, it might get away, go back, and shoot Annie.*

P'Nut pressed harder into his turn. For a second, he lost sight of the drone.

It had sped up even more, but it had also had trouble slewing to the side. P'Nut fired again. A tree stood directly in front of all of them.

The drone hit the tree and exploded. The missile hit the tree and exploded. P'Nut rolled straight up. He flew into the smoke. P'Nut felt the bottom of his platform scrap the tree trunk before he rolled away from the tree and slowed to a stop. Annie floated around the tree with Izzy.

Bond said, "Annie needs to go faster. The robots are flanking your position."

P'Nut relayed the information, "Annie, you have to go faster."

"Okay."

"I'll go first. Follow me."

P'Nut swerved around the tree with the fresh burn scar. He accelerated across an open area. The ground rose ahead of him. *We've almost made it to the hill. We'll be safe.*

A couple dozen robots ran in front of him with their weapons raised. P'Nut hit the EMP button. His fur stood on end. The robots all collapsed. P'Nut sighed in relief. *If that silly bear has stayed safe, I've managed to protect all of my responsibilities.*

Chapter Nineteen

Disaster and Unlikely Heroes

Two types of energy are potential and kinetic. The boulder resting on top of a cliff has great potential energy. A boulder falling or flying through the air has great kinetic energy. Pushing the boulder off the cliff applies force to the boulder increasing its energy and changing the potential energy to kinetic energy.

May you always have the force you need.

Pooh and Eeyore walked between the trees. The river burbled peacefully to their left. *What should I do to help my friends? There'll be robots.* Tree branches rustled above him. Pooh moved slower. He heard a branch snap. Pooh stopped. He looked to his left and saw Eeyore. *It's just him. What will I do about the robots?* "Oh, bother."

Eeyore asked, "What's wrong? Am I making too much noise?"

The little bear scratched his head. "No. You're not making too much noise."

"Then, what's the problem?"

"First, there'll be robots. I'm scared of them, and I don't know what to do about them."

Eeyore said, "That does sound bad. The squirrel said he was frightened. He also said he wouldn't let fear live his life. I'm afraid of the robots too, but I agree with your squirrel friend. I won't let fear

182

stop me."

Pooh said, "That's the spirit." The little bear started walking again. At first he walked fast. *It's all good to go help friends, but I should have an idea of what to do about the robots.* "Oh, bother."

"What's wrong, now?"

"I still don't know how to defeat the robots."

"Maybe there will only be one. I defeated one. I kicked it."

Pooh looked in amazement at Eeyore plodding along with him. The little gray animal didn't look very dangerous. "Just kicking it defeated it?"

"Well. I had help. A bird pooped on it, and a boulder hit it."

"A bird pooped on it?"

"Yes and the robot stumbled and fell into the lake."

"Wow. That defeated the robot?"

"No, but it did slow it down. I kept expecting to die."

"What defeated the robot?"

"The boulder smashed its head."

"That would do it." The sight of the bridge reminded Pooh of something. His stomach rumbled.

"Your stomach is noisy."

"Yes. It is. I think it wants some of the fish over there." Pooh pointed to the other side of the river and his feet led him onto the bridge.

Eeyore asked, "Are your friends going to wait for you to help them?"

"What? Oh. I don't think we have time for me to get some of those fish."

"How soon do we need to help your friends?"

Pooh scratched his head again. "I think we're going to slow. I better go faster." Pooh lifted himself off the ground.

Eeyore said, "What are you doing?"

"I can make myself float. It's a faster way to travel." *Annie could take others with her.* "Eeyore, I might be able to make you float, too. If I can, is it okay with you?"

"It will probably scare me, but if that's how we can help your friends do it."

Pooh thought of when he'd seen Annie lift others off the ground. Eeyore lifted up beside him, but Pooh flipped upside down.

Eeyore asked, "Is it better floating upside down?"

"No. It feels funny." Pooh flipped right side up.

Eeyore said, "You're right. It feels funny."

Pooh looked and flipped Eeyore right side up. The world turned upside down for the little bear.

Eeyore said, "This isn't helping us move faster. I don't think we're going to get to your friends in time to help."

"You're right. I'm having trouble trying to make both of us float."

"Maybe, if you had just one thing."

"What?"

"Set me down, back on my feet."

Pooh carefully lowered Eeyore to the ground. Pooh flipped

184

himself right side up and lowered himself to the ground.

Eeyore said, "Come over here. Stand close to me, and put your paw on my neck. Lift us up together."

Pooh floated them up into the air. "This is better. We better hurry." The little bear thrust his other front paw forward and said, "Charge! We are coming to the rescue."

~**********~

Something red moved behind a tree. P'Nut had a suspicion about who hid, waiting for them.

Annie said, "P'Nut, can you make these other robots fall down."

P'Nut looked away from the tree. Two more robots ran from between two trees. P'Nut shifted his paws lower on the grips. He squeezed a different trigger twice. Differently-shaped missiles, fatter ones, spat out of their ports. Flames burst from them and they sped at the robots.

One of the robots lifted his long thing and fired.

P'Nut tipped the nose of his platform up to block the shot. He didn't hear any ping. He dropped the nose and saw the two robots shaking. The two missiles had clamped onto their sides. The robots fell to the ground. "We're safe Annie. Go up the hill."

No one answered. P'Nut turned around. Annie, Izzy, and the little girl lay on the ground.

A voice drew him away from the disaster. Grace had stepped out from the trees. She held the same thing that had caused the gorilla such pain.

185

P'Nut narrowed his eyes. He watched Grace. She had a finger on a trigger of the device she held. *How long will Annie and Izzy be unconscious?*

"P'Nut, I thought there was more to you than met the eye. You are quite the secret agent. Who do you work for?"

The little squirrel remembered one more trigger on his grips. He'd have to shift his grip down to it. *I can do it. I'm so much faster than humans. But what will happen? I didn't read that part of the instruction video.* "Why does it matter who I work for?"

Grace smiled. "I would like you to work for me. It would be a shame to destroy that wonderful craft you are on."

P'Nut moved one paw up to brush his fur. At the same time, he shifted his other paw down to the third trigger. "Grace, I'm insulted. You like my hardware more than my fleshware."

"Of course I like hardware best. The fusion of hardware and fleshware makes something much greater than the animal."

"Why haven't you fused hardware to your fleshware?" *I need time for Izzy and Annie to recover.* "I saw the gorilla. I know what you're doing to animals. It's despicable."

Grace laughed. She reached up and pulled her hair away to reveal a metal cap. "I have added hardware. I just hide it from dumb, technophobic people." She pointed at her head. "This is the future. I am helping make it happen. My creations and other people's creations are moving us closer to a wonderful future."

P'Nut repeated his earlier comment. "I saw the gorilla. It wasn't happy with what you did."

Grace shook her head. "The most of the poor animals don't take to the enhancements very well. Plus, they don't obey me. I provide help in the form of positive punishment and averse conditioning. If that fails, I by pass the problem by establishing positive hardware control over the fleshware. This is all for the establishment of a better future."

For a moment, P'Nut didn't understand. Bond spoke to him. "She's using pain to control them, and if that doesn't work, she puts them under the control of the machine."

P'Nut shuddered at Bond's words.

Grace spoke. Her face had a real gentleness to it, and her voice had the sound of concern. "P'Nut, what's wrong? This is all for their benefit and for the greater good. They become part of a glorious army that will liberate everyone from their weaknesses. If you're bothered by the pain the gorilla suffered, worry no more. I've decided to skip the use of punishment and conditioning. From now on, we will go directly to positive hardware control. We aren't jealous of our power. We plan on everyone becoming better. There will be no more crime, no more want, and no more dissension. Everyone will work together in harmony."

The little squirrel's earlier bravado vanished as he considered her contradictory words. They painted a scene of terror. Everyone would be locked in their minds, only able to watch what they did. He shuddered at the evilness of her plans. P'Nut was utterly speechless.

Grace's expression hardened. P'Nut noticed her eyes flicker to the side. He heard a soft noise.

Pfft.

P'Nut pulled the trigger. Something streaked at Grace. P'Nut leaned to the side and started tipping the platform. Something flashed just over his body.

Grace ducked, but she'd reacted too slowly. The device streaking at her hit, and she collapsed onto the ground.

Pfft.

Where is that one?

P'Nut flattened himself down. He felt something strike him. Darkness and silence swallowed up his awareness.

~**********~

chapter

Two robots stepped out of the woods and examined the situation. One spoke, "Grace is down. Protocol 'protect Grace' has been initiated. We must return her to base and guard her until she recovers."

The other robot said, "All other robots are returning to base. The aerial watcher has been released."

Together, they moved to Grace. One of them scooped her limp body into its arms. "I will return our master to base. Her better part is still functioning. It says her flesh will recover soon."

A humming-buzzing sound caused the robot to turn. Something very small darted at them.

"I am the fearless Fuego. Fear my sword."

The other robot pointed at Fuego. "What are you? I don't see a sword."

"Enough! I have a sword. See it. Fear it." The humming bird darted at the robot's head.

A strange sound came from the point of the conflict. The robot and Fuego fell to the ground.

The robot carrying Grace turned at a soft noise behind it. The flying platform carrying the squirrel lay on the ground. "Grace wanted the platform and the squirrel. What should I do?"

~**********~

Wind blew past Pooh. He opened his mouth and let his tongue hang out and blow in the wind. *This is fun.* The whole valley lay in shadows. Light from the sun still illuminated the top of ridge to his right. There was a reddish hue to the light. *It's going to get dark soon.* Waves spread over the surface of the long lake in front of them. "Where should we go? I don't see anyone."

Eeyore said, "There's activity straight ahead of us. I see one robot walking on a road toward the bad place. It is carrying something or someone. You need to get us closer. There are other robots, and all of them are moving toward the bad place."

The wind blew faster. Tree tops sped by below them. "Can you see the P'Nut's flying platform, Izzy, or Annie?"

"There's a bunch of metal stuff scattered on the ground. I think it's a bunch of destroyed robots. Wow. P'Nut must be awesome. There's something on the ground ahead and to our left. It's close to the bottom of the hill. What do Izzy and Annie look like?"

"Annie is a big, black dog, and Izzy is a dark-skinned, young woman with black frizzy hair. Do you see them?"

"There is something else or some people closer to the hill." In a louder voice, Eeyore added. "Look out! A big bird is coming at us."

Pooh spotted something flying toward them. It looked like it could be the eagle from Aneroid Lake.

The bird came closer, and Pooh squinted to see it clearer. *Oh, my. This bird looks a bit strange. I don't think it's the same eagle.*

189

Eerie, sapphire light radiated from the feathers on its chest. It tipped its head toward them. Light reflected off the top of the big, brown eagle's head. Pooh's eyes widened. *The top of its head is made of something similar to the robots. What should I do?*

The bird screamed a warning. "Stay away from this area!"

Eeyore spoke with a tremor of panic in his voice, "I think I see Annie and Izzy. This eagle frightens me."

Pooh asked, "What area is that?" The little bear dropped them down closer to the tree tops. "Eeyore, where are they?"

The eagle screamed, "Go back."

Eeyore spoke quickly, "Ahead and to the left, by the base of the hill. Don't let him hurt me."

Pooh looked up. The eagle plummeted at them. Wicked six inch talons glinted as they reached out to slash them. *Those talons are not normal.*

The little bear did the only thing he could think of. Pooh screamed.

Eeyore screamed.

The eagle screamed.

As they all screamed, Pooh and Eeyore continued forward, but they still dropped lower and slower. Pooh couldn't take his eyes off the deadly talons. He felt tree branches brush past them. The eagle crashed into one of the branches and sliced it. The cut end of the branch fell off.

Pooh dropped them lower past more branches. Other pieces of branches dropped from the furious eagle. Pain tore Pooh's attention from the eagle. He'd run into a bigger branch.

Eeyore must've been hit, too. "Ow. Pooh, please stop us, but don't let the eagle get us."

Maneuvering carefully, Pooh dropped them lower between the branches. From above, the eagle's voice didn't sound as loud or as dangerous. Pooh's feet touched the ground. He sighed in relief.

Eeyore plodded away between the trees. "Annie and Izzy are this way."

Pooh heard the eagle's last threat. "I can't get you, but I'm calling for robots to take care of you."

The threat and his fear of the robots sped Pooh's paws across the ground. Eeyore must've heard the threat. He ran even faster than Pooh. "Eeyore! Wait for me, please." The little bear ran as fast as he could. Eeyore ran between the trees and disappeared.

Under the massive trees, Pooh couldn't see as good, but his nose still worked. He smelled something burnt. His nose led him to something metal and plastic, burnt, and lying at the bottom of a big tree. The burnt odor smelled fresh. Another burnt smell came from higher on the tree. *What happened? I think they were chased.* Pooh left the puzzling debris and followed Eeyore's scent trail through the darkening forest.

Pooh heard the rustling of branches from behind him, and he stopped. Quietly, he asked, "Who's there?"

No one answered. Pooh heard another rustling sound. The little bear backed against the tree. "Are you a robot?"

Still nothing answered. Again, Pooh heard rustling, but this time he saw branches waving in the breeze. The little bear let out a sigh of relief. *I better go after Eeyore. He might need my help.*

Pooh let his nose guide him. The trail led him around more trees, across a road, and through bushes. Ahead of him, Pooh saw an open area.

Eeyore called back, "Pooh, I found Izzy and Annie. They aren't moving, but they're breathing. What should we do?"

"Is there any sign of the squirrel, P'Nut?" Pooh kept trudging along.

"His platform is on the ground, but P'Nut isn't there."

"Oh, bother."

Eeyore asked, "What's wrong. Isn't it good that we found them?"

Pooh walked around another tree and some bushes. He saw Eeyore looking back at him. On the ground by him lay Izzy, Annie, and the sweet little girl named Grace. "It is. I just don't know what to do about the squirrel."

Another voice said, "Hello."

Pooh jumped, tripped, and fell to the ground.

Eeyore said, "Hello, Owl."

The owl said, "I saw everything. Those two were shot. The brave little squirrel talked to Grace. He shot Grace, but a robot shot the squirrel. A crazy hummingbird attacked one of the robots. Incredibly, the bird destroyed the robot. The hummingbird is over there. It is okay. I think it needs to warmup. I'm afraid the other robot took your squirrel to the bad place. I hope he wasn't your friend. There is no escape from the bad place."

Chapter Twenty

Final Choices

For some, being a hero is getting up to go forth again even when depression and fear weighs on them like bags of wet concrete. For some, it is ignoring the cuts of the unkind words and deeds to live a life of love and caring. For others, it is not listening to the crowd but seeking what is right, doing the right, and not what is popular. Many of these are the unsung heroes. They don't get medals. There was no moment of glory, just a continual struggle to be who they would be-could be.

Then, there are those whose instinct is not to run away from danger. Running from danger is normal and wise. Those heroes don't think of what is wise. For others, it is giving their all, even their lives, for those they love, friends, acquaintances or just because they believe in the cause. The greatest act of heroism is in surrendering all, not just in the moment, but with premeditation, that others might have hope for a better future. These are those who are most often remembered. Let us also remember the unsung heroes and help each other to be heroes.

Pooh followed the owl through the trees. He had to carefully maneuver around some of the trees. It had been easier with just Eeyore, but now he moved a mass of Eeyore, the three girls, Fuego, and himself. *If only I could move them separately without losing control and spinning them upside down.*

Eeyore said, "I'm getting close to this tree."

Pooh shifted the mass of floating people a little the other way. He tried to ignore the sounds of the tree branches. *They're just moving in the wind.*

Eeyore said, "If we're going back to rescue P'Nut, we need to go faster."

Pooh's stomach grumbled. Pooh agreed with it. He was hungry, frightened, and tired. Pooh heard a snapping sound. *That sounded like a tree branch breaking. This wind isn't strong enough to break branches.*

The owl called from above, "Come up here."

Pooh heard something from the other direction.

Eeyore said, "One of the girls is starting to move."

Right in front of Pooh, the way looked good for a decent distance. Pooh looked up and then, the way he wanted to go. "Oh, bother." He muttered.

The little bear carefully guided the mass of himself and the others up and between the tree branches. Pooh slipped past the last branch and spotted the owl standing on a swaying tree top.

The owl took wing. "Follow me. We should be safe, now. Go as fast as you can."

Gladly, Pooh obeyed. The wind felt good on his face. The sky looked darker. *The sun is setting.* "Eeyore, who's moving?"

"The little girl with no legs."

Pooh and the mass of people caught up and passed the owl. He felt the owl swoop down and land on his arm. His talons pinched but didn't hurt. Pooh said, "Grace, everything's okay. You were caught by a robot, but we've rescued you."

The owl said, "I don't mind if I catch a ride. You're doing great."

I better hurry up. If Grace wakes up in the air, she'll be frightened. I might lose control of my stack of passengers and drop some of them. Below, Pooh first spotted the bridge, then the cabin. "Grace, stay calm. You're being very brave."

Pooh hurriedly moved them toward the cabin. *I'll bring them down in the grass by the cabin.*

A voice interrupted his concentration. "This is fun. I dreamt I was flying, and now I am flying. Weeee."

Pooh shook his head at the surprising girl's spirit. He brought them all down above the grass. Pooh paused just above the ground and slowly, carefully moved each one from the mass and gently lowered them the last feet to the ground.

When Grace settled to the ground, she complained. "I wasn't ready to stop flying. I want to do it more." The little girl's body lifted just off the ground and fell back.

Eeyore asked, "What are you doing?"

Grace answered, "I'm using magnetism to push my body into the air, but it isn't working very well. I can't force magnetism to work very good on something living. If I'm a good girl, can you take me flying again?"

Eeyore laughed. It almost sounded like braying. He said, "Pooh is the one who can take you flying, but right now we have to go rescue our friend, P'Nut."

Grace said, "Let's go."

Pooh looked at Grace and at Izzy and Annie. "We should stay and protect our friends."

The owl said, "Well, well. I guess I can watch over them while you go rescue you other friend."

Pooh's stomach grumbled. "We should eat first."

195

The owl said, "That place down by the lake is terrible. They do horrible things to anyone they capture."

Eeyore asked, "Isn't P'Nut your friend?"

Pooh didn't want to answer the question. He didn't like how he felt about P'Nut and the idea of talking about it felt worse. Pooh remembered his foster parents calling him a hero. *P'Nut isn't a bad person. I shouldn't dislike him.* His stomach grumbled again. Pooh patted his stomach. "Eeyore, you should stay here. This is going to be dangerous."

Eeyore jumped and landed right beside Pooh. He laid his neck over Pooh's shoulder. "You are the only friend I have. I can't let you go be yourself."

"Thanks Eeyore. I think you going to be a great friend. Grace, you can help the owl watch for danger."

Pooh felt a strong little hand grab one of his legs, and then another hand grabbed his other leg. Grace said, "I'm not letting go. I can help rescue your friend."

"But, but the robots."

Eeyore said, "I beat a robot before. I had lots of incredible luck, but I survived."

Grace said, "Robots are made with metal."

Pooh said, "So?"

"Some metal responds very well to magnetism."

Pooh looked at them. He nodded his head. "Bye, Owl. We're off to be heroes."

The three brave souls lifted off the ground and sped back toward the lake.

Grace said, "We're super heroes. Look out villains. Your doom is on the way."

Eeyore said, "P'Nut was right. It is much better not to let fear run your life. I'm still afraid, but this is fun. I might have trouble or get hurt, but I'm trying, and it's fun."

Pooh looked down at Grace. With one hand, she held his leg, but she clenched her other hand and thrust it forward into the wind.

The little bear looked toward the bad place at the head of the lake. In the growing darkness, Pooh saw lights. Moonlight sparkled off the waves of the lake. *This is beautiful.* Lights moved along the shore where the road ran. *What's going on there?* Another light caught his attention. An eerie sapphire light shined in the darkness. It moved toward them.

Grace asked, "What's that?"

Eeyore answered. "It's an eagle. He's very dangerous. It has something glowing on its chest. What are we going to do?"

Grace asked, "Is the glowing thing metal?"

Pooh answered, "I don't know, but it has metal on the back of its head."

The baleful glow soared closer. The light grew brighter. Pooh asked, "I'm going to take us back down into the trees. The eagle can't fly down there."

Sweet Grace said, "No, I've got this."

Suddenly, a squawk filled the air. The sapphire light dimmed. Pooh heard the eagle speak. He could barely make out the faint words. "I'm free. Finally, I'm free."

They left behind the dimming sapphire light.

Eeyore said, "We're coming, P'Nut."

Grace said, "Look at me. I'm a super hero."

Pooh looked down. The little girl had let go of Pooh's other leg and had both arms thrust forward into the wind. *She could fall. No, I've got her, and I've got Eeyore.* The night wind gently caressed him. *It's so peaceful.*

Pooh nodded his head. *I think we can do this. Grace is amazing, and somehow Eeyore defeated one of these robots by himself.* Pooh thrust his two front paws out into the wind. *We are super heroes.*

At that moment, a wolf howl broke the peaceful silence of the night. The howls echoed through the night. "Weasel, we are in position. We are in position."

Wolves? Oh, no. Not wolves, too. Pooh asked, "What are we going to do about the wolves?"

Eeyore answered, "I fought a wolf before. They can be killed. Remember, we can't let fear control us. We have a friend to rescue. Fear would stop us from trying. We have to keep trying. We are trying to live. That means doing things, good things."

Nervously, Pooh nodded his head. *I scared away two wolves before. They aren't that scary.* He remembered the scary, crazy donkey. *Now, that would be truly terrifying.*

The wolves howled again. "Beware the crazy donkey. Beware the crazy donkey."

Pooh shuddered. *I don't need to be reminded.* His heart beat loudly in his ears. *I shouldn't think of the crazy donkey. We'll be okay.* He remembered trying to run from the dream donkey and falling.

Grace said, "We're almost there. I can see in the windows. There are lots of cages. We're going to rescue them."

At that moment, Eeyore said, "I'm not surprised the wolves think

I'm crazy."

Pooh held his breath. Time seemed to pause. At the distraction, their forward flight slowed to a stop. They hovered over a small basin with steep slopes and a small pond that filled the bottom of the basin. *What did Eeyore say?* "Eeyore?"

"Yes, Pooh? What's wrong?"

"Are you a donkey?"

Eeyore answered in a matter of fact voice, "Yes. Of course I'm a donkey. I'm the crazy donkey the wolves are howling about."

Pooh screamed.

The three of them tumbled through the air and splashed into the water. Pooh got up on all four paws. He saw Eeyore coming out of the water toward him. Pooh whirled and scrambled up the slope. He slipped and tumbled back. Someone said something, but Pooh didn't listen. He scrambled up the slope and tumbled back again.

A terrified cry for help cracked the hold the terror held over Pooh. "Help, me." Grace repeated the call, "Help me. I can't swim. Eeyore is trying, but I need help."

Panting with water running down his face, Pooh looked back at the pond. Eeyore stood in the water trying to drag Grace to safety. His hold on her clothing slipped. The little girl splashed back into the water.

Her last cry cut off. "Help—"

The horrible terror of a moment ago felt very small and insignificant. Pooh wailed, "No."

The little bear reached out for the little girl. Pooh knew he could move things. He didn't know how, but he knew. He found her body and lifted her clear of the water and to the shore. He wrapped his front legs around Grace's shivering form. "I'm so sorry."

199

The little girl coughed and spat out water.

Eeyore plodded through the water and mud. His head hung low, and his ears dragged in the water. "This is all entirely my fault. I'm bad luck. I never had a friend before, and I messed it up."

Grace coughed again.

Pooh said, "No, it's my fault. I'm just a silly, little cub. I'm clumsy, I get frightened, and I do stupid things."

Eeyore said, "Nothing ever works out good for me. I should've expected this would happen. It's my fault. I'm bad luck. I'll leave."

Grace finally caught her breath. To Pooh, what she said felt like a slap. "You two idiots. Look at me. I don't have any legs. All I have are two useless flipper-like feet attached to my butt. Do I let that stop me? Yes, Pooh. You are silly, clumsy, and easily frightened, but you're so much more than that. No, Eeyore. You are not bad luck, but you are the most woebegone person I've ever met. Still, Eeyore, you're so much more than that. You just talked about keeping trying. That's what it's all about. We could wallow in what we are or what we can't do, but that's ridiculous. I refuse to do that and both of you should refuse to do that to. Sure, you will be silly, clumsy, easily frightened, sad, unlucky, and all kinds of other things."

She ended her rant with a yell, "Look at me! I'm legless, but I refuse to be identified by my leglessness! I am more, so much more, than that!"

In the silence, after her rant, Pooh heard running footsteps above them. The running steps stopped. The bear looked up. The silhouettes of four robots looked down at them.

The silhouettes smashed against each other, splintered, and flew apart. The pieces crashed to the ground.

Grace said, "I'm crazy. I'm frighteningly crazy."

~**********~

Eeyore felt himself lifted into the air. He looked at the others. Grace floated beside him with her arms out straight, and her hands clenched into fists. Pooh floated on the other side of her.

Together they landed on the top of the slope. Metal started moving around and snapping together.

Eeyore said, "Pooh, I'm glad I'm scary, frighteningly crazy to the wolves, but I'm not scary for you. I'm your friend."

Pooh answered, "Yes, I know. I let my imagination get carried away. I—"

Grace's voice interrupted. "Great. Let's save P'Nut."

Eeyore looked at Grace. She stood straight up. Grace had slapped together pieces of the shattered robots and made a suit of metal that held her up. "Yeah."

The crazy donkey charged the house. A big porch wrapped around the front of the building. Light poured out from big windows illuminating the porch. Eeyore ran up some steps and onto the porch. He whirled at the front door and kicked out with his hind legs. The door crashed in.

Another crash sounded.

Pooh soared in over Eeyore. The donkey whirled around. To the side of them, Grace hadn't waited. She'd ripped out the big window and had started climbing in.

Automatic machinery buzzed. Creatures in the cages called out for help.

Over the hubbub, Eeyore heard two voices. They weren't loud, but he'd been listening for them.

"What's happening to my kingdom?"

"Pooh and Eeyore, you guys came to my rescue? Who's in the metal suit?"

Two robots flew across the room. They crashed together. Their parts went flying. The big window behind them shattered.

The evil Grace stood up in the mess. She held her fists clenched and screamed. "No, no, no. This isn't happening. I rule this place. Where are my robots, my androids?"

A growing roar came from out over the lake. The broken windows left by the destroyed robots revealed the lights of a big plane landing in the lake.

The evil Grace said, "Ha, now you're in trouble. My allies are here. My base here is terribly important to them. I'm harvesting the amazing number of animals in this area that can play with physics. My allies will help me."

Eeyore stood looking at the big thing out on the lake. *It's a plane.* It had landed and moved through the water. Eeyore knew where it went. *She's right. Those others will be here soon.*

The room had fallen quiet. On one side of Eeyore, the amazing child Grace stood facing the evil Grace. On the other side, Pooh stood with one paw out. He looked at something. Eeyore followed his gaze. The little squirrel, P'Nut struggled up onto its hind paws.

Grace snatched him up. "This rat and everything in here is mine. Leave here, and if you're lucky, you'll get away before my allies arrive."

P'Nut said, "I'm not a rat." He bit one of her fingers.

Grace screamed and snatched up a bloody looking knife. She

swung it at P'Nut.

The three heroes all said, "No."

Eeyore tried to run and help. His hooves thudded loud on the hard wood floor, but they also slipped, slowing him down. Eeyore didn't know what he would do. *Bite her? Twirl and kick her?*

He slipped again and bumped into a table. It tipped over with a crash.

Before Eeyore could get to the evil Grace, the knife flew out of her hand and stuck to a metal object on the ceiling. Her fingers wrenched, one at a time and with a popping sound, off P'Nut.

P'Nut fell to the table. "Your allies will not get here in time to save you. Surrender or else."

The evil Grace laughed and said, "You can't defeat me. I will repair my laboratory, my robots, and resume helping animals and people to become better." In a more sinister tone she added, "All of you will become better tools for me."

Sweet Grace said, in a surprisingly grim tone for such a young child, "You'll never hurt another animal." She picked up a chair and hurled it at the evil Grace.

That Grace ducked. The chair tumbled out the broken window.

The big, overturned table lifted into the air and flew at the evil Grace. She turned and jumped out the broken window. The table crashed onto the floor where she had stood. The evil Grace yelled at them. "I will be back."

Sweet Grace said, "My head is killing me."

Chapter Twenty-One

What Now?

It is good to have friends. It is very nice to have friends in high places.

Eeyore turned to sweet Grace. Her exoskeleton slowly collapsed, dropping the little girl to the floor. Eeyore asked, "Grace, what happened? Are you okay?"

Pooh answered, "No. She isn't okay. I'm not either. Lifting that table and throwing it almost killed me."

Eeyore asked, "How? I don't see any wounds. Why's Grace's head killing her? Can we stop her from dying?"

Pooh said, "My head is killing me also. That's what happens when someone plays too much with the laws of physics." He headed towards sweet Grace.

The little bear tripped on robot debris and fell to the floor.

Eeyore asked, "Pooh, are you going to die? What's going on?"

P'Nut jumped to the floor and said, "They aren't dying. Their heads hurt. Thanks for the rescue, but I think it's time for us to leave. If the evil Grace gets back before we are gone, some of us might die and all of us will wish we weren't here."

Grace said, "I'm sorry, but I need some help. Maybe you should leave me."

204

Pooh slowly stood back on his hind paws and walked over to the prone, little girl. Bending down, Pooh scooped Grace up.

Eeyore walked to the shattered door. With each step he heard something new crunching under his hoofs. "We did a pretty good job of destroying her kingdom."

P'Nut said, "Yes, but now she's furious, and she'll be coming back with her allies. Move faster. We need to leave."

Pooh asked, "Can't we release these animals from their cages?"

P'Nut answered, "I'm sorry. I would love to, but we need to leave as quickly as we can. You and the girl were awesome, but you're both wore out, and we really need to be going."

Grace asked, "What about that big red button on the wall."

Eeyore turned to look at it.

Grace said, "The sign under the button says 'emergency release of all the captives.'"

Pooh ran over to the wall. Grace slapped a small hand against the button. Immediately, all the cages clanged open. All kinds of creatures started climbing out of the cages. Grace said, "You're free."

P'Nut said, "Great. Now, can we leave?"

Eeyore led the way toward the destroyed front door. He paused to take in the amount of damage his hooves had done. A noise caught his attention. His ears swiveled, looking for the source. "I hear something."

Sweet Grace said, "Of course you hear something. The freed animals are leaving."

P'Nut said, "Hurry up. We've got to get out of here."

Eeyore ran out the door. "There are noises coming from the

road."

P'Nut scampered across the room and jumped onto the porch.

Eeyore ran across the porch and down the stairs. *Going down the stairs is much harder than going up them was.*

P'Nut ran ahead and from behind, Eeyore heard Pooh coming with Grace. Eeyore also heard, from different directions, noises growing louder. *I think we need more friends. We're outnumbered.*

The massive pine trees stood as dark shadows against the bright stars in the night sky. The rising moon illuminated the tops of the tallest trees. To Eeyore's left, lights moved out on the road. *That's the road from the other end of the lake. Who would that be?* "Some people are on the road to the left."

Pooh said, "That isn't the direction of the big airplane."

Eeyore's ears swiveled. He'd picked up more noise coming from the other direction. "P'Nut was right. I hate to be negative, but we needed to get out of here, and I'm afraid we're too late."

The sound of motors came from the right. Eeyore turned to Pooh. "Can you lift us out of here?"

The noises from the left grew louder. It sounded to Eeyore like the beating of many hooves.

Pooh rubbed his head. "Sorry, I tried to lift P'Nut and failed. Maybe we could hide down by the little pond."

Big vehicles rumbled out on the road from where the plane had gone.

Eeyore asked, "Do any of you have more friends who can help us?"

P'Nut yelled. "Head to the pond. If we can stay hidden long enough, Pooh and Grace will recover. I'll try to make a plan."

206

From the safety of Pooh, sweet Grace pointed up into the night sky. "Look, I think the crazy old man is coming to rescue us."

Eeyore said, "I think we still need more friends."

P'Nut said, "What?"

Eeyore looked at what Grace pointed at. A bizarre platform of logs, carved timbers, and wheel chairs carrying kids dropped from the night sky. An old man stood in the middle of it. Eeyore said, "This is better, but I still think we need more friends."

A light shone from the lead vehicle on the road. A voice came from it. The evil Grace said, "We have you outnumbered. Surrender."

The old man thundered, "They will not surrender!"

Grace said, "That's the crazy old man. I think he's mad. He's my friend." She waved. "Hi."

The sound of hooves grew louder. A large group of horses and riders charged out of the darkness. They carried torches and guns. A voice called out, "Pooh, where are you? We're here to help."

Pooh said, "Mom, the vehicles came from the big plane. They are threatening us. They're evil."

Evil Grace said, "I still have you outnumbered. Surrender."

Bond's voice spoke. "P'Nut, help is arriving right about now."

Dark shapes blocked out the stars. A voice shouted from above. "Everyone, we're friends of P'Nut. All enemies of P'Nut drop your weapons." Ropes dropped and dangled in the air. Armed soldiers slid down the ropes.

Evil Grace shouted, "Retreat!"

Eeyore told Pooh, "I like your friends."

Author's Note

Thank you for joining me on this journey with Pooh, Eeyore, P'Nut, Fuego, Annie, and Izzy.

Before you read any farther, please use the QR code below to write a book review of *Pooh and Eeyore* on Amazon. I would greatly appreciate your taking the seconds to support me in this way. Book reviews are very important to the success of authors getting their books to other people.

Author's Final Note

Hello, everyone. I'm author, TLW Savage, otherwise known as Tim. My real name is Tim Walker. I borrowed the last name of Savage from an ancestor of mine. It gives me a much more unique pen name and will make it easier for you to find my other books.

I hope you've enjoyed this novel "Pooh and Eeyore" as much as I enjoyed creating it for you. I hope the story touches you the same way as the first book in this series, Tuffy, touched other readers. Their reviews also touched my heart. One fan got just what I labored for all of my readers to get. I have striven to give you a delightful mix of heart, humor, and adventure—a book that will stay with you for a long time.

My plan is to create another story in the next six months continuing on from this one, but everyone knows the best laid plans of men and mice often go astray. I will do the best I can.

Below are two different ways of contacting me. I'm still answering all of my email. Also, for any of my fans with ideas they'd love to see in future books please share your thoughts. If I use your ideas, I'll give you credit for the joke, character or whatever the idea was.

You're all amazing, and it was my privilege to share my story with you. Take care. I love you.

TLWalker@TLWalkerAuthor.com is my email

TLWalkerAuthor.com is my website. I'm planning on making a major upgrade to it as soon as I can afford it. Find me on Facebook as: TLWSavage. Be sure to message me on Facebook and identify yourself as a fan. I use to work in Cyber Security, and I'm careful about accepting new friends on Facebook.

TL Walker, Author

Tim began writing in Olympia, Washington. A grandpa, he and his wife enjoy their children and grandchildren. He loves making great food and gets even more enjoyment from watching family and friends eat the food.

He began creating stories at an early age. One night, his seven-year-old sister woke screaming, and he went to comfort her. On the spur of the moment, the twelve-year-old Tim created a fantastical story for her, calming her with attention-grabbing details.

Tim's fascinated by everything from flowers to Genghis Kahn and from sand to the universe. He finds people particularly interesting. He's always on the watch for interesting features and personality quirks for use in a story. If you come to his website and visit, you might find yourself in a book. He has been active in local writing groups and a beta reader for other writers.

Currently, he is also leading Writer Camps. He loves helping others.

www.ingramcontent.com/pod-product-compliance
Lightning Source LLC
Chambersburg PA
CBHW032115020726
47494CB00007BA/2084